EPIPHANY II
LOSING MY SOUL

ANDRE'A T. ROBINSON

DEDICATION

This Book is dedicated to all those who never stopped believing in me, and pushed me to never give up. Whether it was purchasing the books, writing a review, encouraging me, or simply telling me you were proud of me. I Thank you all from the bottom & top of my Heart!

CONTENTS

EPIPHANY II

ACKNOWLEDGMENTS

I COULDN'T EVEN START THIS BOOK WITHOUT ACKNOWLEDGING THE ONE WHO PLANTED SEEDS OF VISIONS AND IDEAS FOR THESE BOOKS IN MY MIND.

LORD, I THANK YOU FROM THE TOP AND BOTTOM OF MY HEART, NONE OF THIS WOULD BE POSSIBLE WITHOUT YOU.

CHAPTER 1

DEAD...WRONG

SKY

As I stumbled up the stairs, I couldn't believe what just happened. I would never ever even consider killing someone. Let alone, touching a gun but, the situation I found myself in proved otherwise. I still had the smoking gun in my hand when I made it outside the house and onto the porch. My entire body was shaking uncontrollably as I walked to the lake which was located alongside of the house. I bent down, placed the gun beside me, and looked at my reflection in the water. Moments later, I started feeling sick. That uneasy feeling was followed by me regurgitating in the water. My heart was beating rapidly as my mind was running a mile a minute? *How would I explain this to the police? What if they assumed I killed C.J. in an act of vengeance? Would I go to jail? After all, I could have easily been accused according to the scene of the crime. What would I tell Lil Carter?* I was dumbfounded. I had no idea what to do next. The thoughts were flooding my mind. In fact, it became almost impossible for me to think straight. I kept telling myself *to get it together...and keep it together.* I was in desperate need of rational thoughts.

I knew the first thing I needed to do was dispose of the

body...*but how?* That's when I had a revelation! *I would just burn the damn house down!* Immediately, I picked up the gun and threw it out into the lake. I knew if someone found it, there would be no finger prints on it to trace it back to me or Dre.' I paced back and forth trying to think of how I was going to torch the house but, then I noticed a shed on the other side of the house. I prayed there was gasoline in it.

DRE'

I touched my chest and back to make sure I wasn't hit. I was relieved that I kept my bullet proof vest on always but, I was sore all over. It felt as if I was struck by a bus and left for dead. Oddly, my arm felt like It was on fire. When I looked down at it, I noticed that it was blood soaked. I looked around but, there was no sign of Skylar. I figured she was long gone until I saw a shadow walking by the house from the basement window. I could hardly get up because I was so sore from the impact of the bullets that must have knocked me out. I wasn't sure how many times she shot me. There was no way to tell. *Thank God, she shot me in the back and arm, and not my head.* When I finally gathered the strength to get up, I limped over to the window to see if she had gone. Much to my surprise, she was coming out of the shed with a can of gasoline. *Fuck!* I thought. *She's going to burn the house down where she assumed my dead body was located.* I gathered myself and prepared to leave the house. I went upstairs to the window that wasn't boarded up before Skylar made it to the side of the house. I needed to go unnoticed. I soon realized that my gun wasn't in the basement, so I knew she must have had it. I hurried around to the other side of the porch, just missing Sky. There wasn't anything in the backyard to hide me other than my old tree house, so I climbed in and watched Sky out of the small window. She was crying hysterically as she poured out the gas all around the house; including the porch and inside the window we both escaped from. I knew this house that I once upon a time called home was old and would certainly burn fast. As I watched her, I could see the terrified look in her eyes. I couldn't believe I was feeling any inkling of remorse for her. After all, the bitch did shoot me! *Yes* but, I did; it was something about her that I loved and couldn't let go of but, I knew the game and point of my initial mission. I also knew that being emotional was not a part of the plan. The bottom line was that when I found her again, I would have to kill her. There were no ifs, ands, or buts about it.

SKY

To my surprise, there was a huge can of gasoline sitting next to an old lawn mower, so I grabbed it. My trembling hands poured the gasoline around the house, outside on the porch, and inside the window. After I was done, I threw the gasoline can inside the window. *Fuck! I didn't have any matches, nor did I have access to a lighter.* I looked up at the two cars parked in front of the house; the one I came in, and the one Dre' had driven. I wasn't sure if there would be any matches or a lighter in them but, I prayed to God that there would be. First, I walked over to the car Dre' was driving and tried opening the door. The noise of the screaming alarm startled me. *"Shit!"* I jumped. The doors were locked and Dre' had the keys, which meant I would have to go back inside and face what I had done all over again.

Next, I walked back up to the porch and climbed back inside the window that I went through before, trying not to get any of the gasoline that I poured in the window on me. I walked toward the basement stairs across the creaky floor. Although I knew I was the only moving body in the house, I was still petrified. I stood at the top of the stairs to listen for any movement. I'm not sure why but, I felt like I was being watched. I looked down the stairs but, I couldn't see anything. I walked down a couple of the stairs. I was shocked to learn that Dre's body was no longer there. The spot where I shot him and watched him fall was vacant. Once again, I felt as if my mind was playing tricks on me. I was immediately panic stricken. I took my phone out of my pocket and turned my flashlight on, and then I shined it around the basement but, I didn't see any sign of Dre.' *Where did he go? I shot him six times and watched him fall. There was no way he could be alive.* I knew that I needed to get something to burn the house down quickly. I was sure C. J. would have a lighter in his pocket, so I slowly walked over to the chair C. J.'s lifeless body was sitting and dug into his pockets. Just as I assumed...he had a lighter. There in his pocket was also his phone. I pulled it out and put it in my pocket. I cried at the thought of not being able to call him again. I cried for Lil Carter. Before leaving, I kissed C. J. on the cheek. *"Rest Peacefully."* Although he had taking me through hell with all the beatings, I felt sympathy for the sake of Lil Carter because he would not be able to see him anymore. I ran back up the stairs and climbed out of the window. The whole time I was there, I was shaking with fear because I had no idea where Dre' could have gone. I literally felt like this was a waking nightmare. My shirt got caught on the window causing me to fall to my knees on the porch. After I got up, I ran around to the front of the house where the cars were parked, and the car that Dre' had driven was gone. *What the fuck? Is this a sick joke? How could he still be alive?*

I paced back and forth on the porch. I knew I still needed to burn the house down to cover up my prints and blood *from* the bullet that grazed me. So, I ran back around to the window, flicked the lighter, and threw it inside. The flames ignited quickly and spread rapidly throughout the old house. I ran to the truck, got inside, and hurriedly started it up; relieved that I decided to leave the keys inside. I pulled out onto the road and looked out of the rearview mirror at the house. It was burning much faster than I expected. There was a cloud of smoke. I knew by the time someone across the lake saw it, I would be long gone. I looked back and thought to myself, *Good-bye Carter.*

<u>Dre'</u>

When I stepped inside my condo, I sat down on the couch. I couldn't believe this was happening. I was angry at myself for even getting involved with Sky. I thought of possible things that sounded credible that I could tell Mr. Santiago...or if I would tell him anything. *Fuck! If I was unsure before, I knew now I would have to find Sky and kill her. The reality was that she knows too much.* I remembered the GPS tracking I had on the Range Rover that Sky was driving. I was hoping she drove it from the house. Otherwise, *how else would she get away from there?* I went to my lap top and opened it. When I did that, a shooting pain crept down my arm and into my hand. I knew I had to go see my private doctor to get that bullet out of my arm before it caused any damage but, that was the least of my concerns. I logged into my GPS tracking, typed in my plate number to the Rover, and it brought up a map. It showed that the truck was on Wyoming and Fenkell St just sitting. I thought immediately that she must have abandoned the truck. I worried and wondered how she was getting around. I needed a plan...and I needed it fast.

<u>SKY</u>

I knew I had to get rid of that truck. I thought about all the cameras and intercom systems that Dre' had in his condo, and his Grandmother's house. I realized that he knew exactly where his truck was. I called my cousin and had her meet me on Wyoming and Fenkell St where I left the truck parked at a gas station with the keys inside. I ran over to the Tim Hortons down and across the street, and waited for her to arrive. Again, I paced back and forth and looked out of the window to make sure I wasn't followed. My hands were shaking badly. One of the employees of the Tim Hortons walked up to me while my back was to her, and touched me on the shoulder. I jumped.

"Hey! You seem nervous. Is everything ok? Would you like for me to call 911?"

I'm sure I seemed confused. Especially when I looked at her as she was staring at my blood-stained shirt.

"No, I'm fine. I just got into a little accident; that's all. It was nothing too serious." I said and smiled so that the girl didn't get even more suspicious than she already was. "Where is your restroom?" I asked, trying to appear calm.

The girl pointed me in the direction. I quickly made my way over there trying to avoid eye contact with her and the other people in the restaurant looking at me. When I got to the rest room I locked the door and paced back and forth. I was losing it. I was trying to seem normal...more like myself but, my mind was still cloudy. I couldn't maintain my thought process. I sat me and C.J.'s phone on the counter in the bathroom and looked at myself in the mirror. Tears rolled down my face. I had never felt so alone and fearful. *What was it that I've done so bad to be punished like this?* My life seemed like it only got worse with time. I thought about the epiphany I had when God spoke to me. I remembered Him saying that I needed to have faith in Him. I did...well at least I thought I did but, why would he be punishing me like this...to this magnitude? I started to feel sick, so I leaned myself over the toilet and threw up. This was the second time that day. I assumed my stomach was upset based upon everything I saw. *Who wouldn't be sickened by the sights?* Abruptly, I remembered I hadn't had a menstrual period that month.

I looked up at the ceiling, closed my eyes, and prayed, "*Lord, I know I don't always do things right and according to your will. I know I sin...I am fully aware. Why is my life this bad? Is it something you're trying to show me? What could it possibly be that you want my attention this badly? Lord, first my Dad, then my Mom, Grannie, and now C.J. Lord why??"*

I began to cry uncontrollably. I felt like I couldn't catch my breath but, then my phone rung, so I got up from the floor. I figured it was my cousin calling because she was outside the restaurant. I looked at my phone to find it was a text message from a number that I didn't recognize.

Skylar, you have no idea what you've done. Can't we just sweep it all under a rug? I tried to save you from all of this but, you couldn't mind your business and trust me. You had to snoop around and come to that house. Well, now you know what must be done. See you soon, my Love.

I couldn't believe he had the guts to text me. *How was he so certain I hadn't gone to the cops with everything that I knew?* I panicked because this confirmed that he wasn't dead or even badly injured, and then I thought, *maybe I should. I will tell them the truth. There's no way they wouldn't believe me but,* that thought quickly left my mind because I wasn't sure who I could trust at this point.

I grabbed C. J.'s phone and walked out of the rest room. When I made it up to the front of Tim Horton's, I saw Theresa's car. I ran to her car as fast as my legs would carry me. I was relieved when I saw that Lil Carter was in the car. I immediately got in the back seat and hugged him tightly while crying nonstop. "Drive!" I said to my cousin. She saw how upset I was, so I was sure that she knew I must have found C.J. dead. I had her drive me to my credit union so that I could empty my account and close it. Afterwards, I gave her the key to my storage unit and had her drive me to the airport. I bought two tickets to Atlanta for Lil Carter and I. I hugged Theresa and promised her I would call as soon as we touched down. I needed to get out of Michigan fast. I felt like I couldn't breathe. The devil was having his time with me.

CHAPTER 2

REIGN

REIGN

I watched her on the security cameras as she approached the customer service counter at the airport. Skylar went off the radar for about four hours. In fact, we thought we lost her until a signal and audio came through from her cell phone. She sounded distraught as she tried explaining, through tears that she needed someone to come for her in a hurry to a Tim Hortons on Wyoming and Fenkell St. After watching Skylar for the past 2 months, I grew to feel sorry for her. The level of my empathy had increased over that short period of time. Going into this case, we thought she was just someone that Dre' was dating until we found a girl dead that was connected with Skylar's boyfriend, C.J. who is now missing. We also came to find out that a case that we had closed due to no evidence or suspect found in 1996, was the murder of Skylar's father. We later put the connections together but, we had no evidence to pen Santiago to the murder. At least not until we came across Skylar McDaniel. I wondered how deeply involved Skylar was in this. On the other hand, her innocence was in question.

"Special Agent Reign will be on assignment with the

girl," we all listened as our lead agent Roberts spoke.

"Reign, I want you to get as close to this girl as you can. Do whatever you must. Use every measure necessary to achieve the ultimate goal...whatever it takes to get her to trust you," he said.

"The Cabrera Cartel is ran by Camilo Santiago. He is a very dangerous man. We've spent several years trying to apprehend him but, he seems invincible. Nothing ever sticks. He has federal agents and judges on his payroll but, we recently got him on a phone conversation with one of his hit men, Dre.' Our thanks go to this girl; Skylar," Roberts said.

"So, what is our approach to this girl"? I asked

"You will be on that plane to Atlanta that she is boarding, as the co-pilot. I want her to see you as just that. We will plan to have you bump into her somewhere in Atlanta. She will be immobile, initially. I'm not sure if she knows anyone in Atlanta. So, we will be following her the entire time. Reign, your job is to make her trust you. She knows a lot because she's running. We just need to know how much she knows, and where C.J. is," Robert said.

As everyone packed up to leave, I sat for a few more minutes watching Skylar in the security cameras. She kept her son close to her but, would move whenever he moved. She looked around constantly. *What do you know, Skylar? I thought.*

I walked through the terminal to board the plane with the pilot. Besides him and one of my colleagues;

special Agent Olivia, no one knew who I was. Inquisitively, they just assumed that I was a student piolet. That was good enough for me. Olivia would be on the plane with us as a student flight attendant. Those were my eyes on Skylar while I was in the cock pit. Every passenger, including Skylar and her son, finally boarded and we took off.

CHAPTER 3

WHAT BETTER PLACE THAN THIS!

SKY

I felt safe and relieved after we finally boarded the plane. The flight wouldn't be long to Atlanta, so I figured I would get a quick nap, until Lil Carter started asking questions. "Mommy, where are we going? Where's daddy?"

When he mentioned C.J....it all hit me like a ton of bricks. I could feel the tears well up in my eyes. I could hardly speak; I didn't know what to say to him. "Take a nap Carter." Taking a brief pause, "When we land and get settled, we will have a talk... ok?"

That was all I could think to say now.

"Ok, Mommy," he responded. He then laid his head across my lap and fell fast asleep. I leaned my head back on the head rest, looked up at the ceiling of the plane, and then out of the window. We were up in the clouds. What better place than this to have a conversation with God.

"Lord; that question that Carter asked me...well, I will definitely need your help with that. Lord, please give me wisdom on the words to use when having that conversation with him. Please Lord, make him

understand even though he is young. Give him the strength to carry on without his dad."

After that, I drifted off to sleep, and into a dream. In the dream, Dre' and I were standing in a field. After looking around, I saw that we were surrounded by water. There was a glass wall separating us as we stood there staring at each other. He looked as though he was lost. And then his expression turned cold. Just as if he was right next to me, I heard him whispering in my ear. Strangely, his mouth never moved but, I could hear him clearly.

"You have a part of me, so now you belong to me."

I was confused at what he said. When I went to open my mouth to ask what he meant, his expression looked as though he saw a ghost behind me, and he backed away from the glass. At that moment, I felt like someone was indeed behind me. When I turned around, there were hundreds of people; both men and women that looked as if they were dead, and they all were staring right at me. My heart felt like it was going to jump out of my chest. Standing in front of the crowd of people, there was a man that favored Dre,' and then there was C.J. standing next to him reaching out his hand as if he wanted me to come to him. He started walking towards me. He looked just like he did sitting dead in that chair in the basement. I backed up into the glass afraid of what he would do. What I was looking at resembled *The Night of the Living Dead*. They all started walking toward me. Seconds before they were close enough to touch me, I felt someone shaking me. I screamed out of my sleep to see the flight attendant standing over me. When I looked around, the plane was empty. I was perspiring and shaking.

"Ma'am, are you ok? I've been trying to wake you for twenty minutes."

"I'm sorry. I'm fine, thank you. I was having a bad dream." I smiled nervously and stood up. I then noticed that Lil Carter wasn't next to me. I panicked.

"My son! Where's my son? CARTER!" I screamed. When he heard my voice, he came out of the cockpit with the pilot.

"Mommy, Mommy! The pilot said that someday I could fly this plane." He was so excited, and it was a relief to see his smiling face.

"Carter, don't leave my side while I'm sleeping. Do you understand? You scared me." I hugged him tight. I felt sick at the thought of losing him.

The pilot reached out his hand for me to shake. "I'm sorry but, you were asleep when we landed and emptied the plane. While Olivia was trying to wake you, he asked if he could come in the cockpit to see what it looked like. Again, I apologize for startling you. I'm Reign; by the way." he said. I shook his hand.

"Skylar," I introduced myself.

I looked up at his six-foot frame. I noticed how attractive he was. He had a perfect smile.

"Thank you. No, it's fine. I just got worried when I didn't see him."

He eyed the blood stain on my shirt. I looked up at his face. Before I had to make up a lie to explain where the blood came from, I hurried, grabbed my blanket and pillow that I bought in the airport back in Detroit, and walked off the plane. I could feel him watching me. When I turned around for the sake of confirmation, he was. So, I smiled as to not seem nervous, and then I continued toward the exit. When I finally made it inside of the airport in Atlanta; the smell in the air was different...so much more different than in Detroit. I felt relieved. I could finally breathe.

CHAPTER 4

HOME AWAY FROM HOME

I had no idea where Carter and I were going from there. I only knew I had seventeen thousand dollars to my name. I would get us a hotel room for the night, and first thing in the morning, I would go look for us a one-bedroom apartment.

We caught a cab to Lenox Square Mall. Believe me; it was pricey! The ride to the mall was nearly forty-five minutes but, I had to make the trip. I needed to get us some clothes, underwear, and other basic needs. We had nothing to start our new life. I also needed to get Carter something to occupy him before he started asking questions that I still wasn't ready to answer.

Carter was so happy when we got to the mall. He was content because the mall meant toys or new games for him. My first stop was to get myself a shirt to wear so that people could stop staring at the blood stains on the one I was wearing. After about three hours, we were done shopping. We stopped for lunch. While Carter was eating, I googled hotels close to the mall. This caused us to have to catch another cab to the Ritz Carlton in Buckhead. I checked into our room; which was quite expensive but, I wouldn't have it any other way with Carter with me. I wanted him to be comfortable. He deserved that after all we had gone through.

We finally made it inside our room for the evening at around nine o'clock. I drew him a bath. After bathing, he fell asleep halfway through the movie he was watching.

I finally had some time to myself, so I cleaned the jacuzzi sized tub in preparation for my own bath. I popped the cork on a bottle of Mascoto wine I bought from a little store in the mall, poured it into a glass, and then undressed as I sipped my wine. Once I was completely undressed, I looked at myself in the full-length mirror on the back of the hotel bathroom door. I hated what I saw; which was some of the bruises from the last beating that C.J. had given me. The marks were just starting to fade but, at that point, I had new ones from the struggle with Dre' earlier that day. The graze marks those bullets left was starting to sting. So, I opened the bag that had the first aid kit that I bought at the mall, and cleaned the graze marks. Tears formed in my eyes at the thought of my life. After I was done, I stepped into the bathtub. It was at that very moment I wished I had some of those Vicodin pills that C.J. use to keep in our closet back home.

The warmth of the water soothed and relaxed me just a little bit. I turned Pandora radio on my cell phone. Appropriate to the moment, Adele's station was playing. I thought of C.J. and began to cry.

I couldn't believe he was gone.

I cried for him because he was alone in his final

moment. He had been rotten to me but, I knew his heart ached for Lil Carter. I cried for Carter because I knew all too well what living without a father felt like. Carter was the same age I was when my father was murdered. I cried for myself and all that had happened to me. All the new pain opened the wounds from the pain in my past. *Why? Why Lord?*

I thought about drowning myself in the tub to end all the pain I was feeling but, then I thought about Carter finding me and feeling the same kind of pain and abandonment as I felt right in that moment. My crying was uncontrollable; which left me to feel like I couldn't breathe. I prayed, *"Lord, I don't understand but, I don't want to ask you why. I'm at the point that I don't want to live anymore. Have mercy on me and help me find peace. I know that you are working for me and not against me Lord, Amen."*

When I woke up that morning, Carter was already up watching cartoons. I looked at the clock: it was 7:30 am. I felt like I hadn't slept at all. I had nightmares all night about C.J.'s body and of Dre' finding me and killing me. I had the worst headache ever from the wine and the crying all night. When I got up to use the bathroom, I felt sick and had to run to the toilet. I threw up and figured I might have drank a little too much.

The hotel offered complimentary breakfast, so Carter and I got dressed and headed down to the lobby. I wasn't that hungry, so I made Carter a plate. I had a plain bagel and a cup of coffee. I sat Carter at the table closest to the TV in the dining area where he could watch cartoons while he ate. There was a business office that guest of the hotel could use. I used that time to do a little research about Atlanta. If we were going to stay there, I would need to look for some apartments.

"Carter, Mommy will be right in there." (referring to the business office) Eat your food and don't make a mess or talk to strangers." The lady at the desk heard me and we made eye contact. She smiled to reassure me she would keep an eye on him.

"Ok, Mommy."

I went into the business office and logged onto the computer. First, I searched for apartments and cheaper hotels just in case I couldn't find an apartment and, we had to stay in a hotel longer than planned. I also searched for shelters in case I needed them too. I wanted to cover all my bases. I printed out a listing of a couple of hotels, apartments and shelters with the directions to each of them. I didn't want to spend the money I had too fast because it was all we had to start over until I could find a job. I also made a mental note to call Carter's school to tell them we moved and have them send his records. I anticipated enrolling him into a new school, so I was thinking ahead. School would be starting back in a couple of months so I wanted to make everything as normal as possible for him.

After Carter was done eating, we took a walk to the local pharmacy; the drug store that was a couple of blocks away. The very first thing I got was a pregnancy test. After I had thrown up so many times, I knew that it wasn't just stress. There was no point in me fooling myself. I hadn't come on my period since about a month prior. Originally, I figured it was from stress. I was suffering with morning sickness. I certainly did not need, nor did I want to be pregnant. I hadn't had sex with C.J in months so I knew if I was pregnant, it was by Dre,' and that would be even more complicated than what I was already dealing with.

CHAPTER 5

WELCOME TO THE ATL

I searched for a prepaid credit card so that I could set up an account with Uber after learning that catching anymore cabs was out of the question. It was much too expensive. I couldn't find them, so I asked the store clerk for assistance. I guess she picked up on my accent, so she asked with a welcoming smile. "Where are you from?"

She was extremely short with girlish looks. I wondered if she was even old enough to work there. I hesitated for a minute because I wasn't sure who I could trust after that text message I got from Dre.' Even though I knew there was no way he could have found out I was there so soon after all that had taken place, I wasn't sure of the kinds of connections he had so to be safe, I lied. "Ohio," I smiled.

"Is this your first time in Atlanta?"

"No. I have a lot of family here. I actually come down a lot." I tried to sound as honest as I could to cover the *half-truth* that I was telling her.

"Ooh! Ok. Cool. The prepaid cards are right here. If you need help with anything else, just let me know," she said in a southern accent as she walked away.

I knew I was being paranoid; she was just sparking up conversation to be polite. After getting Carter some snacks, I went to the counter and paid for the items. I loaded four hundred dollars on the prepaid credit card to be safe. I would look for a used car to purchase once we got settled. After leaving the pharmacy, my baby and I sat on a bench right outside the store. I had to wait fifteen to thirty minutes before the money was on the card. So, I downloaded the Uber app onto my phone in the meantime. My Uber driver was an older woman; probably in her early sixties. She was so nice that because she wasn't busy that day, she offered to drive us to each of the apartment complexes and communities I was interested in. She even took me to places she knew were in nice neighborhoods and had top schools. The crazy thing about it was her name was Marilyn...just like my mother's name. I regarded that as a good sign. She was even playing gospel music in her car. At that point, I felt even more relieved and relaxed. She took me outside Atlanta, about forty minutes from the mall, to Jonesboro, Georgia. We pulled into some apartments named The Lake Villa's.

"This is where I live. I think you would really love these. It's quiet, clean, and in a good neighborhood." Marilyn said.

I looked around when we pulled in and it seemed nice. By this time, I was tired of looking. Most of the apartments in Atlanta were too expensive. These were seven hundred dollars a month for a one bedroom which was all Carter and I needed at that time. We went in and I filled out an application. I was approved within a couple of hours. Marilyn had spoken to the property manager and told her that I was her niece that had just moved to Atlanta. I wasn't sure why this lady was going out of her way to help me but, I was extremely grateful. I shouldn't have been so trusting granted everything I'd been through 48 hours prior but, the vibe I was getting from Marilyn was positive. In fact, she had the same name as my mom, so...

I loved the apartment, so I signed a one-year lease, put down the deposit and paid up my rent for four months. I thought we would be good until I could find a job or clients for my cleaning service. She informed me that there wouldn't be an apartment available for twenty more days, so I would have to wait for my move in date.

It was getting later. When we finally made it back to the hotel that evening, it was five o'clock. I was exhausted and so was Carter. He had fallen asleep in the car on the way to the hotel. "Thank you so much Marilyn. You have been a life saver today. Is there any way I can repay you?"

"No honey, of course not. This was no problem. Are you guys going to be ok in this hotel until your apartment is ready?"

I knew what she was thinking because the hotel was very expensive...and she knew it.

"Yes ma'am. I paid for two nights. Tomorrow, I will try to find somewhere cheaper until the apartment is ready."

She had a concerned look on her face, so I knew she probably wanted to ask me questions about why I moved there. She may have even wanted to perhaps question where I got the money to pay for two more nights at the hotel AND pay the deposit on an apartment with four months rent in advance but, I wasn't about to tell this lady my life story. After all, I did just meet her. She seemed nice and trustworthy but, my guard was up big time.

"Ok, Skylar! Well, here's my direct number. If you need a ride anywhere, don't hesitate to call. My husband works days, so I usually have a lot of free time all day until he gets home around seven pm. I can also speak with him about letting you guys stay with us until your apartment is ready. I mean...we *are* going to be neighbors," she smiled and nudged me.

"Aww Marilyn, that is so sweet of you but no, thank you. I don't want to intrude. Besides, I just met you and all. I mean, I like you. In fact, you are very nice but, with Carter, I have to be cautious... you know?"

I looked back at Carter who was sound asleep in the back seat. I didn't want to put him in any danger, so I *had* to be very careful.

"Ooh, I understand honey. I have a son. Although he is thirty-eight years old now, he is still my baby." She smiled and handed me the card with her phone number on it.

I looked at the card and it read; "*Free Life Church,* Church Secretary Marilyn Evans." I thought to myself *Free Life;* just the kind of life I dreamed I'd have.

Marilyn sensed the sadness as I looked at the card.

"Skylar, God will help you through whatever it is you're facing. Talk to him. I would love to come and get you and Carter Sunday to be my guest," she suggested.

I looked up at her with tears in my eyes and I thought, *if she only knew.*

"Ok, I will give it a try. I will probably be switching hotels, so I will be sure to let you know where we're staying. Thank you so much again, Marilyn."

I got out of the car and opened the back door to get Carter. I had to wake him up because there was no way I could carry him...not with pain in my back. I was already starting to get aches. I made a mental note to find a doctor so that I could get medication for the pain. It would be for my back paired with the pain I was feeling because of all the stuff I was going through and what I had seen and done. I also had to take something for the nightmares. Although, I dreaded sleep, I knew I had to have it.

My poor baby was still sleepy when we finally made it to the room so, I removed his clothes and put him in the bed. I sat my new lease and all the paperwork on the night stand. Although I was weary, I walked to the bathroom and turned on the shower. Just the thought of the hot water touching my body eased my mind. I took off my clothes and stepped in the shower. The water was so soothing. I felt alone, even though I had all I needed in my life; which was Lil Carter but, I was all the way in another state away from my family and friends. I knew no one. I couldn't call my friends or my family because they would question my whereabouts. For their protection and mine, I thought it would be best that I disappeared. The only person that knew I was gone was my cousin Theresa. My secret was safe with her because she had packed her things and moved to Texas with her dad. She knew too much which caused her to be just as afraid as I was. We promised that we would only text every few months so that we knew each other were ok. I couldn't hold back the tears; I was emotionally overwhelmed as I thought of my Mom and Grandmother. The tears wouldn't stop but, I had to put my game face on. I knew that I had to be strong for Carter. I had no other choice.

I got out of the shower after washing up, and put on a long Pajama shirt. Finally, I turned on the TV and sat down on the bed. I was sure to be quiet, so I wouldn't wake Carter.

CHAPTER 6

SIGN OF THE SINFUL

When I looked on the night stand, I noticed C. J.'s phone was there. I had totally forgotten that I removed it from his pocket. By now, it was completely dead, so I plugged it to my charger. After twenty minutes, it popped on. It was no surprise to me that he had a lock on it for the sake of him and his double lifestyle but, I knew his password because I would look over his shoulder without him noticing in the past when he would unlock it. I went directly to his call log but, I didn't recognize any of the numbers other than his brother's and mother's. I then went through his pictures. There was a lot of photos of him and Lil Carter. Those were no surprise. The thing that surprised me were the ones of me sleeping. I smiled because I knew he took them and probably didn't want me to know. There were pictures of him and a lot of different females but, mostly pictures with the girl that hit me with her car. I stared at a picture of him and her kissing. They looked happy and smitten, which made me sad. He hadn't looked at me in that way in years. Sure, he did when we were much younger but, time had stolen our kindred spirit. Maybe I wasn't completely innocent but, I too had my reasons...

I closed the photos and looked at his text messages. In the receiving were a lot from the same girl that struck me with her vehicle ...Trina. So *that* was the name of the mysterious girl. She wasn't the only one but, she was the only one that sent him naked photographs.

There were more texts to another number I didn't recognize. In one of the outgoing messages from C.J. He said the man's name that texted Dre': *Santiago*. I now knew why he was under the radar, and then murdered. In the last couple of the text messages received, C.J. hadn't answered him back. I went to the notes app and there were a lot of notes reminding himself to do things. I opened one that had my name on it.

Skylar,

I love you and I'm sorry for all the pain I put you through every day. I need help. I promise I'm going to get help. No one loves me like you do, yet I continue to hurt you. I have to leave for a while to get my head together. I did something that could cost me my life. And for you and Carter's safety, I have to disappear to protect you and my son. I promise I will contact you so that you know that I'm ok. Tell Carter that I love him. I'll see you soon.

C.J.

I couldn't stop the tears from falling. I could hardly see, so I wiped my face and read the note over and over. *So, he knew that we were in danger and he didn't tell me?* He never even sent me the note. C.J. wanted to leave to protect us but, he was the one I needed protection from. So many questions went through my head but, I knew that I wouldn't get any answers because now he was gone forever.

The question at that point was, *why does this Santiago man still want me dead? What am I going to do with no one to protect me?*

CHAPTER 7

SICK OF BEING SICK

It was happening again...I started to feel sick. Barely making it to the bathroom, I hovered over the toilet throwing up. When I closed my eyes, C.J.'s lifeless body flashed before them. I felt like I was drowning in my own vomit. I collapsed onto the floor on my back when it finally stopped. I could hear my heart thumping in my ears. I rolled over on my side and covered my mouth to muffle the sound of my unending tears. I didn't want to wake Carter and have him see me like that. I debated whether to go to the police and tell them everything but, I wasn't sure just how connected this Santiago dude was. I was so scared of what him or Dre'; whomever got to me first, would do to me and Carter. I knew I needed to be very cautious...at least until I could come up with a plan. First thing in the morning, I needed to find a doctor. I needed something to cope.

I got off the floor, and brushed my teeth and washed my face. I looked at myself in the mirror and saw my mother staring back at me. I could now see for myself that I looked so much like her. I thought of what she would say to me. I knew she would say she raised me to be stronger than this. Then I thought about the pregnancy test I bought because I had to pee. I went to look for the bag that it was in but, I couldn't find it. That's when I realized I must have left it in Marilyn's car. I was exhausted with everything, so I turned the television off and laid down in bed.

As soon as Carter felt me lay down, he rolled over into my arms. "I love you, Mommy," and then he kissed me.

"I love you more, Carter."

I wondered if he heard me throwing up and crying. I would find out sooner or later because if Carter had questions, he never hesitated to ask them. I soon drifted off to sleep.

CHAPTER 8

LORD KEEP US SAFE

Before I knew it, Sunday had come. I called Marilyn the night before to let her know the name and address of the hotel we moved to. It wasn't quite where I wanted to stay. It was a motel to say the least. I could tell that drug addicts and dealers used this motel to get high and to make sells. I went to Target the day we moved there to purchase cleaning products; bleach mostly. I also bought new sheets, blankets and a padded mattress cover so that we didn't have to use the motels linen. I had heard too many horror stories about how little the staff put into sanitization. I was a stickler for cleanliness. I bought a mini fridge, and a lot of snacks and microwaveable meals. I also grabbed something dressy for Carter and I to wear to church.

After getting dressed, we waited on Marilyn. When she got there, I noticed her husband was with her. He got out of the car and opened the door for Carter and I.

"Hello, Skylar. My wife has told me a lot about you. I'm so happy you decided to join us for church this morning."

"Nice to meet you." I extended my hand to shake his.

"Robert," he offered his name.

34

"Robert! Yes." I smiled and got inside the car.

On our way to church, Marilyn had on a gospel station, so everyone was quiet. Occasionally, Robert would spark up conversation with Carter. He was also a *video gamer* so him and Carter clicked right away. I thought to myself, *what is this old man doing playing video games?* I suspected he was around sixty-five years old but, *I guess for a man you're never too old for video games and sports.* When we pulled up to the church, the parking lot was full. I got nervous because I hadn't been to a church since my mom's funeral. I avoided going because it was something about the sound of the organ. I was always in tears by the end of service. It always seemed like the preacher was talking directly to me.

When we walked in the church, everyone was so nice. They welcomed us with open arms. Robert and Marilyn introduced me to everyone. The church had a *children's* church so that's where Carter went. In fact, he was more than happy to go when he saw all the kids his age there.

Marilyn, Robert and I walked down to the front of the church. I guess because she worked there, she sat up front. There were seats reserved for them. Robert walked up to the alter and took a seat next to who I figured was the Pastor. *To my surprise he was very young.* The praise team was amazing! When they sang, you could feel the presence of the holy spirit. Along with the Pastor, they had everyone jumping out of their seats. Needless to say, by the end of service, I had cried so hard I developed a headache. The Pastor didn't even know me, yet he talked about every single thing I was battling. I prayed hard that morning in service. I was sure God heard me. After service, I met the Pastor. He seemed like a down to earth guy. I also met some of the other members. Marilyn and Robert excused themselves. They had to go take care of some business in the church office. She assured me that it would only take about twenty minutes. I sat in the lobby area of the church and waited as Carter was playing with some of the kids outside in the parking lot. I could clearly see him from where I was sitting. Briefly, looking down at my phone, I decided to delete my social media accounts because I didn't plan on getting on any of them to be safe.

CHAPTER 9

WHEN IT POURS, IT REIGNS

"Skylar, Right?" I heard a deep voice ask.

I looked up at his 6ft frame, and beautiful smile.

"Ummm...Reign, right?" We shook hands again.

"Hi! So, you remember me, huh?"

"Yea! Well, Reign isn't a typical name. and I never forget a face."

"How are you liking Atlanta?" he asked. Then I noticed his southern accent. I hadn't noticed it when I was on the plane when we first met.

"It's been great so far. I met this nice couple that invited me to church."

Moments later, a girl walked up with a look on her face like, *who is this?* She extended her hand. "Hello. I'm Nicole, Reign's girlfriend. Who are you?" She asked with a smirk on her face.

Before I could introduce myself, Reign corrected her and introduced me to her. "Friend. Not Girlfriend." He shot her a look. "Nicole, this is Skylar. I met her on my flight. She was a passenger on my plane."

She stood there and looked at him in surprise.

"Nicole and I work together. She's a flight attendant," he offered.

"Ooh ok. That's cool." I said disinterested.

Reign handed Nicole the keys to his car, "I'll be out in a minute."

She was visibly pissed and walked away.

Reign took my phone out of my hand and dialed a number. Next, I heard a phone ring. Then, he took his phone out of his pocket and hit the end button on his iPhone and handed mine back. "Now you have my number and I have yours," he smiled. "Call me when you want me to show you around Atlanta," and then he walked out of the door.

I started blushing and put my head down. I shook my head thinking about how aggressive the men in Atlanta are. *Every time Carter and I go somewhere, the men don't even care that I have my child with me. They still try to holla at me...and are very persistent when they do.* Although a male friend was the last thing on my mind, I couldn't help but notice how handsome and well-dressed Reign was. He looked like he was straight out of a GQ magazine. His cologne was hypnotizing with just one sniff. I could still smell him even after he was long gone.

Marilyn and Robert snapped me out of my day dream when they came out of the church office with the Pastor. When they reached me, the Pastor extended his hand. "Hello, Skylar, right? Marilyn and Robert told me they brought someone to church with them today. It's a pleasure to meet you. I hope you enjoyed our service today." he smiled.

"Yes, service was amazing. I will be back. Thank you for having me," I said while shaking his hand again.

I was smiling on the way to the car because I was happy that I decided to join them at church that morning. I felt like I had some sense of relief after hearing a word from God. I soaked up all that the preacher was saying and decided that whatever God was trying to tell me, I was listening hard...

I was quiet on most of the ride back to the motel. I just kept thinking about all the things the preacher said about being happy and having peace. I day dreamed of what that would be like. I hoped it would come soon. Marilyn called my name loud over the radio and she turned around in her seat. "Skylar?"

"Huh? Ooh, I'm sorry. I was in deep thought." I said embarrassed.

"Robert and I were going to go have brunch. Would you and Carter like to join us? It'll be our treat."

"Yes, we would love to. I'm starving." I couldn't remember the last time I had eaten anything.

Luckily, the restaurant had booths large enough to lay Carter down. The excitement of playing with the children in church had tired him out. I was sure he would be asleep for a while. After placing our orders, the inevitable had taken place. Marilyn turned to me with a look of concern. I knew the questions would come sooner or later. "Skylar, the place that you all are staying? That motel isn't safe for you and Carter," and then she turned to look at Robert. "You could always come to stay with us until your apartment is ready."

Robert added, "Skylar, I don't know what your story is or what your life has been like but, it was put on Marilyn's heart to help you from the first time you met. She knew she needed to help you."

A tearful Marilyn seemed to be looking right into the windows of my soul; concentrating on the view of my past while Robert continued, "The way you cried in service today let me know that you have been through a lot. We just want to help you and show you the goodness of Jesus."

I looked down at my hands, and started nervously fiddling with them. They seemed like genuinely kind people. I'm sure they meant well but, I couldn't tell them why Carter and I came to Atlanta.

"I appreciate everything, Marilyn and Robert but, we will be fine. Besides, it won't be long before the apartment will be ready. I haven't had any issues yet at the motel. Actually, it seems pretty quiet." I lied. "We will be fine. Again, I thank you. I really do appreciate the offer and concern." The frozen smile I wore was one of which I intended to convince them both.

After an amazing morning in church, and enjoying a scrumptious brunch, we made it back to the motel which was visibly more crowded than it was this morning. There were people hanging out in front, and children playing on the grassed area of the motel. I realized then that it was one of those motels that people live in long term. I said *goodbye* to Marilyn and Robert and hurried myself and Carter inside, not wanting to draw a lot of attention to myself. After closing the door and locking it, I went to the window and peeked out to look at the group of guys sitting across the parking lot from my room. They were drinking and shooting dice. One of the guys was looking directly at me as if he knew that I would look out there at them. I noticed that he was on his phone, He was a short guy with muscles bulging out of his tee shirt. He looked like a body builder but, judging by all the tattoos on his arms and face, and the mean mug he wore, I assumed those muscles came from lifting weights in someone's jail. I looked around the room and my eyes landed on the desk that sat by the window. I pushed it in front of the door, praying that if anyone tried to get in, they would have a difficult time. I leaned up against the desk and closed my eyes. *"Lord, if you are listening, please keep us safe here."* I *prayed.*

CHAPTER 10

KING OF THINGS

KING

"Hey Boss, She's here".

"Good! Keep an eye on her. I don't want her trying to run again. We have her right where we want her," schemed Santiago

"She has a son..." I tried explaining, as if it was going to change his mind

"I don't give a fuck! I want that bastard son dead too! Have you seen or spoken to Dre'?" Santiago asked

"I called Dre' a million times. He's not down here. I can't seem to get in touch with him."

"Ok, I'll worry about Dre' myself. He better not be trying to help this bitch again. You keep an eye on her until I decide when to move. I want her to suffer." Santiago was fuming.

"Ok Boss. This won't be hard at all. I'll catch her when she's alone, and I'll get her to trust me because you know I'm not your ordinary neighbor." I said with a smirk

I don't know what this girl was thinking. She stuck out

like a sore thumb. No women that beautiful would be caught dead in a motel like this. I watched her as she got out of the old couple's car. I was shocked to see that she had a son. Santiago left that bit of information out. I was wondering what this pretty thang did to Santiago that he wanted her dead but, that was none of my business. The less I knew, the better for everyone. I definitely wasn't trying to get on that crazy muthafuckin' Cuban's bad side. My job was simply to watch her and make sure she didn't run, or go to the police.

CHAPTER 11

THE SLEEP OVER

Carter and I stayed inside for the rest of the day. Luckily, we had left overs from the restaurant. Carter was asleep by nine o'clock. I took a shower and went to lay with him. Instead of resting peacefully, I laid awake listening to a myriad of noises. There were cars screeching off, people arguing, and babies crying. I opened my phone to the calendar, *August 9, 2015.* I counted down from the twenty days before the apartment would be available. Soon afterwards, Carter would be starting school, and I could get my life back on track. I was mentally exhausted and emotionally depleted.

I woke up the next morning to the sound of my phone buzzing from a text message. There was a number I didn't recognize but, it had an Atlanta area code. I found this to be weird because no one from Georgia had my cell phone number besides Marilyn whose number was stored in my list of contacts. I sprung from the bed. My fear was that Dre' had found my whereabouts. I thought of the text I got from him before I got to the airport. By now, I was almost too nervous and petrified to open the message but, I couldn't resist. *"Hey, Beautiful! I know it's early but, I wanted to catch you early before you made plans for the day. I would love to take you to brunch and show you guys around Atlanta. Call me when you wake up and get dressed. -Reign"*

I plopped back on my pillow and sighed in relief. *It was Reign. I should've saved his number in church yesterday.* I smiled at the thought of how persistent he was. It was impressive. Then the questions had become*: Should I text him back? Should I let him take us to brunch?* I contemplated my answers because I wasn't so sure I could trust him either. He seemed nice but, so did Dre.' Look where that had landed me. *Maybe I'll just let him take me out to dinner.* Whatever decision I was to make, I was certain that I didn't want to involve Carter. I wouldn't allow him to pick me up either. I'll meet him. I texted him back.

"Hey! Good morning. Brunch? NO. Dinner? YES. Just me and you though." I waited for him to respond.

"Perfect! Can I pick you up around 7:30 pm?"

I didn't want to respond right away so I waited ten minutes. *"Well...I was hoping I could meet you!"* I returned.

"Ok! That's fine! I'll text you the address and reservation time in a few."

I rolled over and smiled but, soon afterwards, my smile disappeared when I thought of having to leave Carter. I would have to leave him with Marilyn and Robert. I trusted that he would be in good hands. A small part of me was apprehensive because we hadn't been in Atlanta long. I had to stay mindful that Dre' wasn't dead and could be searching for me. *Who am I kidding? I'm over seven hundred miles away. He wouldn't even know where to start looking for me, if he is even looking.* I quickly put the thought out of my mind because I knew if I dwelled on it, I would drive myself crazy. So, I decided to call Marilyn.

"Hello Marilyn, is it possible you could watch Carter for me tonight? I was invited to go have dinner with a friend."

"Sure! I would love to have him over; will you be out late? No worries, he can just spend the night. This is great timing because I will also be watching my grandson. He is the same age as Carter!" She was very excited.

"Ooh wow! This *is* perfect timing. I don't want to intrude. He doesn't *have* to spend the night." I paused briefly. "But, if it's ok with you...?"

"Yes...sure, Skylar. As a matter of fact, I'll come get him around 3:30pm because my grandson will be here around that time, and then I'll take them to see a movie."

"Ok, perfect! Thank you so much, Marilyn."

Carter was still sleeping when I got off the phone with Marilyn so I decided now would be the perfect time to catch me some more *zzzzz.* As I laid there, I stared at Carter. He looked so much like his dad. I knew it was only a matter of time before he would ask where his dad was again. Sadly, I still hadn't come up with how or when I would tell him. I needed to take one day at a time for the sake of sanity. I thought about the dream I had every night...wishing it was a nightmare. However, I was often reminded that I was living it out when I referred back to the note I read in C.J.'s phone.

I woke up to the sound of Carter talking to someone through the window of the motel room. I jumped up out of the bed. "Carter, why are you in the window? Who are you talking to?" I yelled as I ran over to the window. The three children ran away. Fearfully, I quickly closed the window and curtains.

"Mom, can I go play with them?" he asked with the sad eyes. I knew he missed his friends and cousin back home. I realized that he has been cooped up in this motel room with me since we got there. I felt bad for him. That was even more of an incentive for me to move mountains to get us out of that motel room but, my hands were tied. We would have to make the best of it. I was relieved that he would have an opportunity to play with Marilyn's grandson later that day.

"No, Carter. I don't want you playing out there. That parking lot is too busy; it's unsafe," I said calmly.

"But, Ma I'm bored. All we do is stay in this room." He hung his head in sadness.

"I know Carter. Mommy's so sorry." I empathized. "We will be moving into our own apartment soon, and you will be able to play outside. Ooh, guess what? I have some exciting news for you." I started tickling him.

"What? What? What is it Mommy?" He asked as he jumped up and down in the bed with enthusiasm. "Is Daddy coming down here with us?"

The look on his face when he thought it was about his dad would've lit up a room if it was dark. I felt so bad but, I didn't want him to see that.

"No, baby." I immediately changed the subject. "Marilyn and Robert are coming to get you in a few hours. They have someone who they would like for you to meet. I just know you guys are going to have an awesome time at the movies!" I was trying to sound excited because I know if he sensed my sadness, he would want to know what was wrong. His smile grew even bigger which indicated that he was pleased, and that I was off the hook for the time being.

"Are you coming too, Ma?" he asked, as he continued jumping up and down on the bed.

"No, Mom has some business that I have to take care of today and tomorrow...so rather than dragging you around with boring old Mommy," I playfully said to him, "You get to have a sleep over at Marilyn's house."

He was so excited that he ran to take a shower and pack himself an overnight bag. He even packed some of his toys and games. Carter was ready and waiting by the door in one hour tops. I knew he was anxious because normally, I would have to force him to shower that fast.

Marilyn and Robert arrived about thirty minutes later. When I walked Carter out to the car, I noticed the guy that I saw outside the day before...staring at me. Although uncomfortable, I smiled politely when we made eye contact. I was sure to keep my eyes on Marilyn's car.

"Hey, Robert! Hey Marilyn!"

They must have sensed my nervousness because Robert got out of the car and looked in the direction of the guy. "Is everything ok, Skylar?"

"Yes, everything's fine," I smiled to change the subject. "Carter is really excited about today."

"Well, we're really *excited* to have him over," Marilyn added.

When Robert got in the car after getting Carter inside and putting his seatbelt on, Marilyn stepped out and pulled me to the side. She also looked in the direction of the *mysterious* guy that was staring at me. "Skylar, I have some bad news. The manager of the apartment building said they won't have your unit available for one more month. It turns out that the tenant decided to pay one more month's rent before he moves. Listen... you can always come stay with us until it's ready. I really don't like the idea of you guys having to stay at a place like this for any longer than you absolutely have to," she said looking around.

That news crushed my world. I was sure to be moved out of this motel by the end of the month. *Now I would have to stay an extra thirty days.* It was time to re-budget my money.

"No, Marilyn it's fine. Carter and I will be *just* fine. Thank you though."

"Ok, Skylar. In case you change your mind...that offer always stands."

I reached in the car and kissed Carter, reassuring him that I would see him the following day. At that time, I went back to my room to get more money to pay the front desk for the extra weeks I needed to stay (hoping this would be my final payment). I was disappointed by the news but, I had to stay focused and remain hopeful that we would be moving soon.

When I made my way back outside, the *mysterious* guy was standing beside his car. After we made eye contact again, I hurried inside the motel office. *"Hello, I'm in room A311. I want to pay for another two weeks please."* The girl behind the counter looked at me as if she was confused. While pulling the file out for the room I was in, *"So, in total...you want an additional month?"*

"No... just for the *next* two weeks." I was confused. *Why would she say one month?*

"Well ma'am, the upcoming two weeks are paid for. Someone named King signed for the payment that was made," and then she put away the file and walked back to the television and continued watching her program. I walked outside...still baffled. *Who was King? And why did he pay for my room for a few weeks?*

I turned to walk back in thinking maybe it was a mistake but, I stopped in my tracks when I heard a voice (with a southern accent) directly behind me ask, "You good, Shawty?" It was the *mysterious* guy that kept staring at me.

"Yes, I'm ok." I started toward my room instead of going back into the office.

"You're welcome!" he hollered.

I stopped dead in my tracks and turned to him. "I'm sorry. What was that?" I asked. "*Welcome* for what?"

He walked up to me and extended his hand. "King."

I was certain he said *King*; the same name of the person that the girl at the desk told me paid for two weeks towards my room. Shaking his hand, "It's Skylar. Umm, thank you. Now, I must ask, why did you pay for my room? I'm not even staying here for two weeks."

"Well Shawty, they will give you the unused balance when you leave. Think of it as a security deposit. I wanted to do something nice for someone. Because you're so beautiful, I chose you," he smiled.

After noticing how cute he was, the mental picture I prematurely painted of him as a mean convict disappeared. *That was the nicest thing ever.* "Thank you, King. That is thoughtful of you. How can I repay you?" I asked politely.

"Let me take you out to dinner or lunch...your pick."

I wasn't expecting that, so I didn't know what to say. I didn't want to sound rude or ungrateful by saying *no*. Besides, I wasn't sure how he would respond to rejection. "Ok, um...lunch would be good...maybe dinner. I must get back with you on a date. I'm new around here, so I'm not sure where to go," I said shyly.

"No, worries. I got you. I've lived in ATL my whole life so I know a few places we can go." He stared into my eyes.

I turned my head, trying not to make eye contact in case he could sense that I was lying. "Ok... sounds like a plan. I'll let you know." As I walked toward my room, I felt as if his eyes were burning a hole in my back. So, I kept walking trying not to turn around.

"SKYLAR!" he called out. I stopped and turned around slowly. "How will I know *when*? Are you gonna let me call you?"

"I've seen you every day over here, right? I'll see you around and let you know." I turned and opened the door to my room. When I closed the door, I leaned against it and sighed in relief. I was nervous and didn't know why. I looked down at my phone and it was already 4:30 pm. I needed to shower and get dressed to meet Reign. Just then, I got a text message from him.

"Steak House Atlanta 1065 Peachtree St. NE, Atlanta 7

pm reservation. See you soon, Beautiful." I read his text.

"Ok, how should I dress?" I responded.

"Casual." he returned.

I smiled and went into the bathroom to shower. I decided I would pull my hair into a simple messy bun. I didn't have much to choose from to wear. Luckily, when Carter and I went to Target, I found a pretty coral Blazer, ripped jeans and a pair of cute nude pumps. Target had some nice items. I also purchased a coral like Matte lipstick that I wouldn't normally wear but, I thought it would complete the look. Besides, I couldn't just let it stay on the shelf.

It was 6:30 pm by the time I finished dressing. I called an Uber; it was there in less than ten minutes. I walked outside and was relieved that King wasn't out there. Little did I know, he was sitting in his car across the street watching me. I told the Uber driver where I was going; he knew exactly where the restaurant was.

"Job interview?" he asked.

"Um no, I'm meeting someone for dinner." *Why would he assume I'm going for a job interview at 7pm?* He looked surprised. I was guessing it was where he picked me up from.

CHAPTER 12

AS I WALK THROUGH THE VALLEY OF THE SHADOW OF DEATH

We finally arrived at the restaurant. "Thank you." I politely said while exiting the car. I fixed my clothes and looked at the time on my phone. (6:59 pm) *I made it just on time.* Reign was already there waiting near to the door. The host lead us to our table. Reign pulled out my chair like a gentleman; something I wasn't accustomed to. When we sat down, the waiter came to take our drink order. *"What will you be drinking tonight ma'am?"*

"I'll have a Hennessey; double shot on the rocks, and a glass of water, please." My nerves were on edge. and I needed something to calm me down. Tonight, wine was not going to do the trick.

Reign looked at me and smiled. I could tell he detected my level of anxiety.

"Hen, huh?" he laughed.

"What? A girl can't drink Hennessey?"

"Nope. You can drink whatever you like." He said with a smile.

When the waiter came back with my drink, I downed it and asked for another one. I knew I needed a boost. Otherwise, I would've been quiet and boring. After a few more drinks, I was relaxed. The food there was amazing. I normally didn't care for steak but, these were the best I'd ever tasted, and I needed to try them just once more.

"So, Skylar, what do you do for a living?" Reign asked.

"I have a home cleaning business. I moved here to expand my clientele." I was forced to lie because I wasn't going to get into why I was there (in Atlanta) because it was none of his business. Besides, I didn't know anything about him other than he was a pilot, where he worked, and where he attended church.

"That's awesome. There are tons of opportunities here. I actually have a few friends looking for a home cleaning service. I'll refer them to you...if that's ok? As a matter of fact, I need one also. I'm always out of town so I never have time to clean..."

"Wow! Thank you. That would be nice. In fact, I'd really appreciate that." I smiled. I needed to start making some money. "So, your friend from church didn't seem so happy about you correcting her about being your...um *friend*?" I laughed. I knew the only way a woman would want to be introduced as more than a friend is if a man gave her a reason to. I was curious about what their story was.

"Ooh! Nicole... yeah. We've been friends for a long time. She would like more than a friendship, but I'm not interested." He looked down at his glass, and then back up at me. I tried to search for any sign of that being a lie. Based on his facial expression, it seemed genuine.

"So, what about you...anyone special? What about your son's father?"

I wasn't ready for the question about C.J. It was evident in how I panicked. *"Excuse me?"* I immediately got up and asked a waitress where the restroom was. After she pointed it out, I apologized to Reign. *"Excuse me. I'm sorry,"* and then I walked away quickly.

Once I reached the bathroom, I went into the first stall I saw open. I closed the door trying to hold back the tears and planted my back up against the door. When I finally was alone, I couldn't hold the tears back any longer. I knew the other ladies in the rest room could hear me because I made no effort to be silent. I couldn't believe how emotional I was from being asked that questions. It was the first time since everything occurred that someone other than Lil Carter had asked about C.J. I was an emotional wreck, and I didn't (for the life of me) know why I felt guilty for what happened to C.J. Someone knocked on the door of my stall. That prompted me to snap out of my thoughts. "Excuse me. Are you ok?" a woman asked.

I pulled myself together, grabbed some tissue and

wiped my face. "Yes, I'm fine. Thank you." I opened the stall door and there she stood. At first, I thought I was looking at a ghost but, that wasn't the case. Dre'a was standing face to face with me. I couldn't believe my eyes but, it was real. I knew it the moment she spoke to me.

"Skylar! Wow! What a surprise!" she said with a smile. I was at a loss for words, and I was a mixing bowl of emotions; scared and nervous all at the same time. I knew that seeing her would mean that Dre' would eventually find out where I was.

"What are you doing in Atlanta? You left so suddenly. I'd asked Dre' several times how you were. He always remarked that you were just fine. I figured with all that going on, you probably needed to be alone and with your family."

At that moment, I realized she didn't know anything about why I was there. Either that or she was a good liar like her brother so, I didn't want to give too much information.

"Yes. I do have a lot going on, and needed to clear my mind. I'm here visiting a friend. I'm actually leaving tonight to go back to Detroit." I had to think fast. I didn't want them to know I was living in Atlanta.

"Ooh ok. Unfortunately, I'm here for other reasons. I'm sorry to have to tell you this, Sky. My grandmother passed. Atlanta is where she was born and raised. In fact, most of our family lives here in Athens so we had her body sent here to have the funeral," she explained with tears in her eyes.

I couldn't believe Ms. Loretta was gone. I began to feel sorry for Dre.' They were close, and I knew she was all he had.

"The funeral is tomorrow. Stay one more day and attend the funeral. You know we will arrange and pay for you another flight with no problem. I'm sure Dre' would love to see you."

Still thinking on my toes, "I'm sorry, I have other obligations back home that I can't rearrange. Otherwise I would." I gave Dre'a a hug. "I hate to leave so soon but, someone is waiting for me. Send Dre' my condolences. Again, I'm sorry." I quickly left the restroom without even bothering to turn around but, I heard her right before I walked out but, then again, I didn't...

"Wait Skylar! Why were you crying?"

When I reached the table, Reign stood up. *"I'm so sorry Reign. I didn't mean to..."*

He cut me off. "It's ok, Skylar. I shouldn't have asked you such a personal question. I paid the bill. Were you ready to go?" he asked.

"Yes." I grabbed my purse and we walked towards the

door. As we were leaving, Dre'a and I briefly made eye

contact. It was peculiar.

"Thank you so much for dinner. It was amazing." (not knowing what else to say)

"Anytime. Listen, I would love to go and have drinks but, I have an early flight in a few hours. I'll be working most of the week. However, my vacation starts Thursday and I'll be in Miami for the weekend. You're welcome to come join me." he smiled.

"Well um..." Before I could make up an excuse not to go, he cut me off. "Don't worry about expenses. I got you." He looked at me in anticipation for my answer.

I smiled and lowered my head. "I will have to get back with you on that. I don't have any family here, so I will need to get a sitter for Carter for the weekend but, I'll let you know." That would be a stretch because there was no one I would be able to leave Carter with while I was in Miami. Although I knew it would be hard, I would think about it.

"Ok, well let me know. Can I give you a ride home?" he asked.

I didn't want him to know that I was staying in the motel I was staying at. "No, it's really on the other side of town, and I already requested an Uber. Thank you, though." I said with a smile hoping he wouldn't pressure me to allow him to drive me there.

"Ok, I'll wait with you. I wouldn't be much of a

gentleman if I didn't." he laughed.

Just then, the Uber driver pulled up. We exchanged hugs. As I walked to the Uber I could feel his eyes watching me. I turned to say *goodbye* but, to my surprise, he was already gone. I guess I was wrong.

The Uber driver was a little Indian man who talked to me the entire ride. He asked where I was from because he must have noticed my accent.

"Michigan, Detroit," I said.

"Oooh, really? I have a lot of family in Michigan." he said. He told me about his family and how he was contemplating moving to Michigan with them. When we pulled up to the Motel, he turned to me with a concerned look on his face. *"Ma'am, is this where you're staying?"*

"Yes. Thank you." I proceeded to get out of the car.

"This is not a safe place for you to stay." With a look of caution; he continued, *"Be very careful."*

"Ok, thank you." I got out of the car. I hadn't even closed the door and he was pulling away. I thought to myself; *what a coward! He should rethink moving to Michigan. Especially Detroit!*

CHAPTER 13
LOSING MY SOUL

I walked toward my room reaching inside my clutch for my key. When I looked up, King and a few guys were standing by a car across from my room. He and I made eye contact. I looked away trying to avoid another conversation with him. It was nice that he paid for my room. He seemed like a nice guy but, I knew he was a street nigga based on him hanging around the Motel every day. It must have been a spot for him. A place where he sold drugs. When I got to my door, I fumbled with the key. I heard one of the guy's yell. *"WHADUP SHAWTY!"* I ignored him and went inside my room quickly. I locked every lock and put a chair under the door handle. I went to run me a bath, I took off my clothes and got ready for my bath. I called Marilyn to check on Carter. When I spoke with him, it seemed as if he was having fun. He sounded so happy. When I was done bathing, I stood in the mirror and stared at myself. I couldn't believe all that was going on. My life had taken a complete turn.

ധ ധ ധ ധ ധ ധ ധ ധ

I heard a knock at the door. I quickly put my pajamas on and went to see who it was. When I looked through the peep hole, I immediately got nervous because it was King. I knew I couldn't pretend I wasn't there because he saw me come in. It was getting late, and I was curious as to what he could possibly want at 12 am.

"Skylar, it's me...King. I was wondering if you wanted to roll with me to my homeboy's party?"

I moved the chair from in front of the door and unlocked the locks, and then I cracked the door open. When I did that he pushed his way through the door. I was totally caught off guard.

"So, you gonna keep playing hard to get?" He said slurring his words. His eyes were blood shot red, and I could smell the alcohol on his breath. I couldn't believe he was being so bold. He didn't close the door all the way, so I tried to stay calm. I knew if need be, I would make a dash for the door and run like hell!

"I would love to go with you but, my aunt is on her way with my son." I lied and looked at my watch. "They should be here any minute." I said it as calmly as I could so that he wouldn't sense that I was frightened. He looked at me like he wanted to rip off my gown. I regretted taking that bath; had I not, I would have been fully clothed. He walked closer to me until we were face to face. He was so close that our lips damn near touched. When he grabbed my waist; I prayed he didn't notice my body shivering with fear. By the way I was shaking, I knew he had to feel it.

"I should just take this pussy." he grabbed my panties and tried to pull them to the side. At that moment, I knew he was going to rape me. He walked towards the door and looked back, "but, that wouldn't be good for you or me." he said with a smirk.

I was confused at that statement but, I didn't dare ask what he meant. It didn't matter because before sunrise, I would have Carter and my things packed, and then leave the motel. Perhaps, he was reading my mind.

"Ooh! And don't try to leave, Shawty. Don't even think about it. All you will do is make things worse when I find you." He walked out the door and closed it behind him.

I fell to my knees breathing as if I was having an asthma attack because I held my breath the whole time he was in my room. *What was that? What did he mean "if I left then it would be worse?" and the other statement... "that it wouldn't be good for him or me?" This can't be happening. NO! Dre' couldn't possibly know I'm here already unless Dre'a called him as soon as I left but, how would he know where I am staying? How! I've seen King every day. Is that why he stares at me? Is he watching me for Dre'? Or worse...Mr. Santiago? NO! This couldn't be!* I secured every lock on the door and moved the big dresser in front of it, and then I turned off all the lights before grabbing my phone and curling up at the top of the bed holding my knees to my chest so that I could hear every movement in the room and outside the door. I wouldn't be going to sleep on this night. I didn't even know how I would get out of this motel because King was there every day.

Even when I didn't see him, there was always some guys sitting in the parking lot. I needed to be careful because I didn't know if he had someone watching me. The sound of my phone vibrating startled me out of my thoughts; unknown number. Although I was hesitant, I answered without saying *hello*. I just held the phone. The person on the other line didn't say anything either. I could only hear breathing, and then I heard his voice. My poor heart sank. "Skylar, I know you're there. My sister told me she saw you. I already knew it. I've been watching you, and we need to talk as soon as possible."

I couldn't hold back the tears or anger. I was tired of hiding and being terrified. "WHY CAN'T YOU JUST LEAVE ME ALONE, DRE'!" I screamed. "I DIDN'T DESERVE THIS. I DIDN'T ASK FOR THIS DRE'! WHY ARE YOU DOING THIS TO ME?"

"SKYLAR, SKYLAR LISTEN!*"* I heard him screaming over *me*. "I know I fucked up. I was confused. I wanted to help you. I love you but, I didn't know what you were going to do after finding C.J. so I had to do what needed to be done to save my own ass. My intention wasn't to try and kill you. I was shocked when I thought the bullet hit you and you were dead. I've had time to think... and I'm sorry. Sky, I love you. I'm in Love with you...and I said fuck Santiago because of you. I wasn't going through with my contract. I didn't tell you about it because I knew you would've told C.J. and gone to the police. Now Santiago wants you and me dead. He knows where you are Skylar!"
When he was done speaking, I couldn't find the words

to respond. I was crying frantically. *"knows where I am? What do you mean? Why does he want to kill me? I didn't do anything I knew nothing about what C.J. Did, he already had C.J. murdered? Why me, Dre'? WHY ME?"* I couldn't breathe.

"Skylar, listen to me. You must trust me. Please! Trust me, Skylar." he pled.

Too much had happened. I no longer knew who to trust. I hung up the phone because I felt sick. I jumped off the bed and ran to the bathroom to throw up. I couldn't believe this was happening. I was so stupid to think that they wouldn't find me.

While sitting on the floor hovering over the toilet, I thought about the pregnancy test that I picked up at the store after misplacing the first one. Dreadfully, I went to get it out of my purse. I knew this was something I had to do because I kept having (not only morning sickness) but, *all*-day sickness. I started praying that it was from all the stress I'd been experiencing. I opened the box and followed the instructions. I sat there and waited the 15 minutes. This time seemed like an eternity. I thought about the last time Dre' and I had sex. We didn't use a condom or even bother to stop when we both met our climax. I was sure it was from that night because I hadn't had sex with C.J. in months...and when I did I had a period several times after that.

I fiddled with my hands; much too frightened to get up and look at the test. When I got the courage up to face my reality, I looked at it and slid down the side of the wall. I couldn't believe my eyes despite the obvious. I already knew because of the symptoms I was having. I was hopeful that it was not the case. *Why can't I catch a break?* There was no way I could have this baby...not by Dre'. Then I thought, *what would he do if he found out I was pregnant with his child? Maybe he would spare my life?*

I didn't believe anything he told me about wanting to help me as opposed to killing me. Those were his last minute desperate attempts to get me to let my guard down and allow him back into my bed and my head. I couldn't trust anyone at this point. I needed to go get some help but, who could I trust? I thought of telling Marilyn and Robert but, they probably would want me to go to the police, and then I thought of Reign. Maybe he can help me get to another state where they can't find me. All those thoughts flooded my mind but, I didn't know if I could trust them with this information. I was exhausted from thinking about these things, so I went back to bed. Before I knew it, I had fallen asleep.

I was awakened by the pounding on my door. I had an excruciating headache. I looked at my phone and there were one hundred missed calls from Marilyn. I jumped up out my bed when I heard her voice screaming my name on the other side of the door.

"SKYLAR, SKYLAR OPEN THE DOOR PLEASE!" She was crying. I ran to the door, moved the dresser from in front of it, and opened it. She was standings there looking like she had seen a ghost. Tears covered her face, and she had blood on her clothes.

"Marilyn! What's wrong?!" I looked around but, I didn't see Carter. I was panic stricken as I walked towards her car. "Where is Carter? Marilyn, where is Carter?" Right away, I noticed the blood on her hands. "What happen Marilyn? WHERE IS MY BABY, WHERE IS CARTER? You better tell me something! Anything!" My adrenaline was on ten. The more she failed to speak; the more I shook her back and forth. No reaction. Marilyn was in shock. Robert stood by the car unable to speak. His eyes were red also. It was apparent he had been crying. I knew, at that moment, something happened to my baby. My heart dropped into the pit of my stomach. My frantic tears turned to rage. "WHERE THE FUCK IS MY SON? WHERE IS MY BABY?"

"Skylar, I'm so sorry. It happened so fast. We were coming out of the restaurant from breakfast and a car pulled up. It all happened so fast," she repeated. "The noise...the bullets. Carter was closest to the car...walking ahead of us. I swear they had to be aiming for him but, he is just a child. Why would they be aiming for him. I keep trying to make sense of this. Carter was hit by every bullet. Why would someone do this. He is just a baby." Marilyn was talking to me, God, and herself.

Robert cried as he slid down the side of the car to the ground. I couldn't believe what I just heard I knew this must be a bad dream and I would wake up in a minute. My heart felt like someone just ripped it from my chest. I screamed so loud all of Atlanta should have heard me *"CAAAAAAAAAAAAAAAARTTTERRRRR! Noooooo My Babbbbby!"* My legs gave out from beneath me. Everything was moving in slow motion. I could feel myself drifting in and out. Robert put me in the car, and then he went and got my purse and phone, and locked up my motel room. He and Marilyn drove me to a hospital. I was cold upon entry. Maybe it was stemming from a part of my soul leaving my body. Robert had given me his jacket because I still had on my pajama gown. There were a lot of police officers there. When we walked in, they recognized Marilyn and Robert and escorted us to a room where Robert sat me down in a chair. A doctor came in and kneeled in front of me. He then grabbed my hands, I knew what he was going to say. With tears in my eyes till I could no longer see, I began to scream. "Please Doctor! Please help him! He is just a baby! Please! I need him! Please! I can't live without him!"

"Ma'am, I'm so sorry. There was nothing we could do. He was shot multiple times. I will need you to come and identify him. The couple over there that came in with him informed us that they were babysitting for you. We need a parent or next of kin to identify him."

I couldn't believe what I was hearing. I felt sick and ran to the garbage can, and threw up. I was convinced that I was being punished. *Why was God allowing all these things to happen to me?* The doctor and several nurses walked me down the long and cold vestibule that lead into a room that resembled an operating room. Robert tried holding me up. I needed any support I could get because I felt like my legs were noodles. A tearful Marilyn stayed behind. She was just as distraught as I was so Robert had to be strong for the both of us. When we finally got to the room, I saw a figure of a small body lying on the hospital bed under a white sheet. There were stains of blood all over. Before the Doctor even removed the sheet, I could feel my legs giving out beneath me. I could barely see through the river of tears that burned my eyes. When he pulled the sheet back just past his beautiful face, I could see his hand hanging over the edge of the bed. Again, my body collapsed to the cold hospital room floor. Robert couldn't hold back his tears as he tried to pull me up. Carter looked like he was sleeping with his hand clinched into a fist. He was probably trying to repel the bullets. He was a soldier...my little soldier. Carter had a small hole in his cheek. My crying increased but, the blooding curdling screams had no place to go. So once again, I turned to God. I bent down with my head almost touching the floor and screamed, *"WHYYYYYYYYYYY LORD? PLEASE BRING HIM BACK TO ME! PLEASE! I CAN'T LIVE WITHOUT HIM, LORD! PLEASE! WHAT HAVE I DONE? PLEASE CARTER WAKE UP BABY! WAKE UP!"* I got up off the floor and laid across the bed cradling him in my arms, just as I would when he slept with me. I kissed him and wiped the blood from his mouth. I looked at him and noticed he had the tracks of dry tears running down his face. I hated myself because I knew that he wanted me to save him and I wasn't there. At that moment, I wanted God to take me with him. I had no reason to live now.

My life was over. I died on that table with Carter that

day.

The police officers informed Robert they were looking into what happened. They believed the shooter was aiming for someone inside the restaurant. They also apologized and said they would do whatever they could to find who did this but, without any witnesses, they wouldn't get too far with the investigation. The hospital kept me over night because Robert informed them that he wasn't comfortable leaving me alone. I was sedated for the night. They had me on suicide watch because I kept waking up from the sedation and trying to get out of bed and break the window. I wanted to jump and kill myself. There was no way I could live without my baby.

Over the next few days, tons of counselors, doctors, police, and people from Marilyn's church came to visit me in the hospital. The pastor of the church prayed over me and told me that the church was going to pay for Carter's burial expenses along with his funeral that would be held at their church. Marilyn and some ladies from the church took care of everything. After three days, I was released from the hospital. Robert came to pick me up and insisted that I go to their home. I didn't have the strength to argue so I agreed to go. I spent the rest of the day in bed crying. I couldn't eat or sleep, and by the end of the week, anyone looking at me could tell. The bags underneath my eyes weighed down my face. I was frail because I couldn't hold down any food. I threw up every day all day.
I couldn't eat anything.
I don't think I was prepared for the out pouring of love

from the people at the church on the day of the funeral. There were three hundred cars parked outside. My knees weakened thinking about having to see Carters lifeless body again. As I walked in, there was a choir singing a song with the lyrics; *"I let go and I let God."* I could hear the sound of the organ playing even through the sound of my wailing tears. Everyone around me was praying and praising God but, that was far from my thoughts at that moment. I couldn't understand why God would be letting me go through something like having to bury my only child. It was one thing to lose my Dad, Mother and Grandmother, and then C.J...but, losing my child, mine, my only reason for living...was something I couldn't grasp. By the time I made it up to his casket, I broke down. I tried hanging on to Carter for dear life. I don't know what came over me. I was taking my baby out of that casket and he was going to wake up because I knew this whole thing was nothing but, a horrible nightmare. As the people at that church pulled me away from him, I knew it was real. My tears continued throughout the duration of the service. I don't even remember anything that was said or done that day. When it was time to close the casket, I screamed, and I laid my upper body over the top of it. That was the last time I would see his sweet face again.

On the ride from the cemetery, I couldn't *feel*. I wanted to be alone. Marilyn and Robert kept trying to convince me that I shouldn't be at a time like this. They were adamant about being a support system for me. I wasn't trying to hear nothing anyone was saying. I just wanted to be alone. They dropped me off at the motel.

It was my first time being back there since the morning of Carter's murder. I walked to my door and looked up at the guys standing in the parking lot doing what they had done every day since I came there; drink and shoot dice. King was looking at me and we made eye contact. He smirked, causing rage to fill my body. All I could think about was what he said the night he burst into my motel room. I knew he was connected to Dre' or Santiago...and in some way, connected to Carter's murder. I was wishing they would just kill me and get it over with because I couldn't...no way and no how...live without Carter.

CHAPTER 14

DEATH BY PRESCRIPTION

When I finally made it inside my motel room, I looked around, and everything was the way I left it. That night, I didn't bother moving the dresser in front of the door like I had done before. I was praying for death. I wanted someone to kill me. That was my answer to it all. I looked around the room and Carters things were exactly where he left them. That kid knew he was junky. I spotted a sweat shirt he had worn a couple days before he died, and I picked it up. When I smelled it, I couldn't hold back the tears. I screamed his name. I fell to my knees and held my head back. When I closed my eyes, I could see Carter lying on that hospital bed with his fist clenched all over again. I cried harder. *Why did they have to do my baby like that?*

My phone dinged, and I got up off the floor to look at the text message. *"Hey, I know you probably don't want to talk to anyone or be bothered right now but, I heard what happened through someone at the church. I'm so sorry I couldn't be there due to work. I was out of town. Skylar, I'm here if you need anything. I mean anything. I'm praying for you. Call me when you can."*

Reign was concerned; yet he hardly knew me. He

seemed like a nice enough guy but...I didn't want to drag him into my mess. I couldn't risk another life being taken on the count of me. I kept blaming myself for all of this, even though I knew it wasn't my fault any of this was happening. It was C.J.'s wrongdoing...running off with Santiago's money and drugs but, why did I have to get involved with Dre'? I would have to hold myself accountable for that. I should've paid attention to those signs...but, I didn't. I cried myself to sleep that night. I silently prayed that I wouldn't wake up.

I jumped up out my sleep that morning because I had that dream again. There I was... standing in the field surrounded by water, and the glass wall separating Dre' and I. I remembered that he said that I had a part of him. I grabbed my stomach. *Could it be that he talking about the pregnancy? Oh, my God! Did he know?* It happened again; his face turned cold, and there C.J. was with other people that looked dead. When they started walking towards me, I noticed that Lil Carter was standing next to his dad. I could see his mouth moving as if he was trying to tell me something...but, I couldn't make out what it was. He tried to reach for me and I tried to reach for him. However, when we touched the glass wall, the ground gave out underneath me, and I fell into (what I thought) was water. As I tried to stay afloat and breathe, I looked down at my hands and it was a sea of blood and fire instead. I woke up in a pool of sweat. My heart was palpitating. I looked over to the other side of the bed and I didn't see Carter. I jumped up as if he was still there but, then reality hit me like a ton of bricks. Carter was gone forever...and I was alone. He was all I had.

I wished death upon myself. Talking to God was something I had learned to do but, I had yet to get an answer back other than when Dre' shot at me and I was passed out. Before speaking, I tried to remember what he had said but, unfortunately, my mind was elsewhere. My pain was so heavy that I thought of the pills that I had taken from my closet that C.J. always kept. I wished that I had those with me at that very moment. I thought of hurting myself, so I could go to the hospital and get a prescription for Vicodin...but, then I thought of the guys that hung out outside the hotel. I knew they would be able to direct me to the right person. I was desperate for relief. I thought about King and wondered if he was working for Santiago or Dre.' At that point, I didn't care. I was willing to put myself in the hands of whoever was looking to kill me. *Make it easier on all of us! I would no longer be hiding. They would no longer be looking, and I could be with my baby again.*

I showered and got dressed, and then I grabbed the envelope I had hidden in a small hole in the wall behind the toilet with the money I had left in it. I grabbed one thousand dollars just in case someone tried to charge me an arm and a leg for the medication. I was buying it off the streets...so I had to be ready to pay *street* taxes.

When I opened the door, the sun hit me in my face and blinded me. My eyes were swollen from crying. I felt like I hadn't seen the light of day in ages. I covered my eyes with my hand. When I was finally able to regain focus, I saw one of the women that stayed in the motel with her children (the ones that were at my window talking to Carter) sitting in front of her door smoking a cigarette. I walked over to her, and much to my surprise, none of the men were around...including King. I felt relieved. I walked over to her and tried to make small talk, making sure that I didn't speak in my normal *proper* voice, so she would be able to relate to me (and vice versa).

"Hey, excuse me. You got an extra square?" I asked. "I'm trying to stop smoking." (smacking my lips between the sentences) "But girl! My nigga stressing me out. He keeps calling me trying to get me to come back home. I left his ass because he don't know how to keep his dick outta other bitches. You feel me?" I hoped I wasn't over doing it, and prayed she didn't see me shaking through my clothes.

She looked me up and down and didn't speak for a minute. "Yea, I got another one but, it's gonna cost you a dollar. Ain't shit free around here." She pulled out a pack of cigarettes from her bra.

"Thanks, girl." I tried not to light it until I walked off but, she offered me a light and a seat.

Shit! I didn't smoke so I hoped I didn't sit there and choke like a damn fool. I just wanted to break the ice

and then ask her if she knew where I could find some

Vicodin.

"Soooo... you from around here? Because I haven't seen you before you came to this place." she said looking at me suspiciously.

I wanted to vent...tell her the truth but, I knew that wouldn't be wise. I was sure she would probably understand because she looked like she had been through some shit herself. Her hair looked like she had that weave in for years. It was beginning to mat. She had on a long t-shirt, and I don't think she had anything under it. She had multiple scars on her legs and arms. Her feet looked like they had never seen a pedicure. The bags under her eyes were starting to make her face look like it was drooping. I couldn't do anything but stare I her. I actually felt sorry for her. She hollered at all the kids playing on the motel grass. There were about five of them.

"Are those your kids?" I asked. I was trying desperately to change the subject from the question she had previously asked. I took a puff of the cigarette and tried not to cough.

"Yes. All them bad ass bastards are mine. Sometimes, I hate being a mother but, every time I try to get rid of them, social services keep giving them back!"

I was in mid puff when she said that. I couldn't help it, so I coughed like I was choking on a bone. Her words brought tears to my eyes because I would give anything to bring Carter back. I felt the tears about to come down, and I didn't want to have to explain to her why I was crying, so I quickly asked her what I came over there for. "I'm sorry. My throat is a little itchy. Hey, question? Do you know where I could buy some Vicodin pills?"

She looked me up and down. "Vicodin? Oooh! That's your fix. Shit! I only take that when I'm trying to go to sleep. I have some of those...and something stronger if you want."

She went into her bra again and pulled out a pipe. I couldn't believe she offered me that like it was a piece of gum or something. She got up from her chair when she saw the look on my face and told me to wait there, and then she went inside and brought out a huge prescription bottle that was full of big white pills. "How many you wanna buy?"

I couldn't believe she had such a huge bottle. I wondered if she bought those off the streets or if she got them from a doctor. Whatever the case...I needed that plug. "How much for the whole bottle?"

She looked at me and laughed. "Girl, the whole bottle gonna cost you a pretty penny. You don't look like someone that has a drug problem."

I wanted to say, *"I'm not. I just want to kill myself fast,"* but, I decided against giving her any details. "I'll give you two-hundred for the bottle." I wasn't sure how much pills cost on the street but, at this point, I didn't care. I would've paid *whatever* for them. She laughed harder. I thought the two-hundred I offered wasn't enough. "Ok! Three-hundred." I said starting to get frustrated because she kept laughing. I wanted to get this over with before King decided to wander back to the motel and see me.

"Girl! Two-hundred was more than I was going to ask for but, if you insist on paying three-hundred, I ain't gonna object. Here you go." She pushed the pill bottle inside my hand.

I reached into my pocket and pulled out the money. I counted three-hundred dollars from the thousand that I brought out my room. Her eyes got big.

"Girl! With all that money, why are you staying in this dump?" She asked giving me a strange look like I was the police.

"I'm just having my apartment renovated and I didn't want to pay to stay in no expensive hotel because I wasn't working with much. You know what I mean?" I asked nervously. I decided to leave at that time because I knew the flood of questions were about to come.

"Well, I have to go. Thanks girl. I have to get back to my room."

Before I made it to my door, one of the kids hollered to me. "Excuse me! Is Carter home? Can he come out and play with us?"
At that very moment, I felt the beat of my heart in my

throat. I stopped in my tracks and turned around. I didn't answer him. I ran to my door and unlocked it. Once I was inside, I dropped to the floor and screamed. "I just wanted my baby back. Why couldn't I just have him? Lord, I will give up anything in this world. Just give him back."

I looked at the bottle of pills that I had in my hand and I opened it. Killing myself would be less painful than what I was feeling at that time.

CHAPTER 15

TOMORROW *MOURNING*

I woke up the next morning, I felt fuzzy. In fact, I couldn't remember anything. I was laying in the bathtub fully clothed. The pill bottle was on the floor. I picked it up to find that there were only three pills left. I couldn't believe that I had taken all those pills in one night. I knew for sure I should have been dead. When I stood up; I stumbled. I could still feel the effects of the pills. I was floating...not walking. I went inside the sleeping area of the motel room. It was dark because all the curtains were closed. The room was a mess...as if it had been trashed purposely. The air was rancid. I soon learned that the reason being was the vomit that lined the floor clear across the room. Opening the window was useless. It was that bad.

I tried to recall the night prior but, it was all a blur. I couldn't even remember where I put my phone. I eventually found it on the bed but, it was lifeless. I plugged my phone up and waited for it to power back on. I had a dozen missed calls and messages from Reign and Marilyn. There were also missed calls from a number that I didn't recognize. I listened to the messages. *"Skylar, it's been days. We haven't heard from you. I know that you are depressed, honey. I know you miss Carter but, you have to continue to live. It will be hard...at times, nearly impossible but, Jesus will cover you baby. You just have to have faith."*

I cried as I listened to the message from Marilyn. She left a few more pleading for me to call her. There was a message from Reign. "Sky? Hey. I've been calling you for days now. Call me. I'm worried."

The last message from Marilyn expressed an even greater concern for me. She said if I didn't call her by *today...*

That's when I realized that it had been a week and a half since Carter's funeral. I had been a sight unseen. It became apparent that the Vicodin pills had me sleeping continuously. I probably was nodding when I was waking up. I couldn't remember the last time I had eaten. I didn't have much of an appetite anyway. but, then I experienced a sharp cramp in my stomach...so piercing that I was doubled over in pain, and then I became nauseous. The pain between my legs prompted me to crawl over to the bathroom and throw up. It all came rushing back in! I remembered that I was pregnant. I took all the pills without giving a second thought to my unborn child.

After I threw up, the pain went away. I was sure I was going to have a miscarriage because of the number of pills I had taken. When I finally got enough strength to get up, I walked out into the room, the motel manager and the girl that sits at the front desk were standing in my door with the look of disgust on their faces.
"Ma'am... what the hell happened in here? You haven't paid your rent for this week...that's why we are here.

Judging by the looks of this room, we should be concerned about more than that. You will have to pay for the damages...aaaaaand you have to leave. We can't have you destroying our property like this."

I couldn't believe he had the nerve to speak to me as if I was in a five-star hotel. He was putting me out of a raggedy ass motel. I didn't have the strength to argue with him. *"Ok, whatever. I'll leave but, I'm not paying you a damn dime for this piece of shit! It looked worse than this when I came here. FUCK YOU! And fuck you too!" I made this suggestion to the both of them.*

I went around the room and grabbed what things I could. I decided against taking all of Carter's toys and clothes. There was no use for them. I only took the shirt he had worn to bed the last night I saw him. I grabbed my money out of the hiding place in the wall in the bathroom, and then I gathered what was left of my clothes. I pushed past the clerk and bumped her.

"You better watch it, bitch! I ain't the one!" she said.

I looked at her, rolled my eyes. and walked toward the entrance of the motel. I saw King and the woman I got the pills from standing next to King's car. They were both staring at me. King was smiling with an evil glare on his face. The woman just shook her head. I looked around for somewhere to sit and pack my things in the duffle bag...all the while thinking of who I could call. It was early. I put my head inside my hands. My life was on a downward spiral. I couldn't catch a break.

CHAPTER 16

I WILL! I WON'T! I WANT TO!

Shortly afterwards, I heard a car pull up. I couldn't see who was inside. By the time, I stood up and tried to walk away, someone came from behind me, placed something over my head, and pushed me inside the vehicle. I was too afraid to scream. I couldn't keep up with what was happening. Things were moving too fast to know. At this point, it was over. Santiago had found me just as Dre' said he would, and he was going to kill me. All I could hear was my own breathing. When the car stopped, something hit me in the head.

When I woke up, I was tied to a chair inside what looked like a hotel room, and my mouth was taped. When I opened my eyes, I was blinded by the light. This prevented me from being able to focus on the figure standing in front of me but, then he spoke, and his heavy accent made me know exactly who he was...the same voice I heard on the phone with Dre' at his condo.

"Skylar honey... you are a very hard person to catch up with. I thought for sure you would be begging me to kill you after my men shot that bastard son of yours." Those words cut me like a sword to the back. I didn't want to believe that they had anything to do with Carter's death. I would rather have been left with the thought that it was a mistake... that he was at the wrong place at the wrong time.

He stood there and stared at me with a smirk on his face. If I hadn't been tied to that chair, I would have kicked his ass but, what would that do? Carter would still be gone. Nothing could bring him back. So, I wished that Santiago would kill me and get it over with. I looked up at him through the tears burning my eyes.

"If it was left up to me, Skylar my dear, I would kill you right now but, because the men in your life were disloyal to me...and stole my money, I have other plans for you. Also, someone wants to say *Hi* to you."

I heard a door open behind me, I couldn't see who was coming through it until he walked in front of me. Our eyes locked, and he stared at me just as he did when we first met. It was the same thing... like he could see straight through my soul but, the expression was different. Before, he wore a look of concern. I was convinced he would never hurt me. This time, it was different. I moaned in anger at the thought of him lying to me that night on the phone. He was still working with Santiago to destroy me. I almost fed into his bullshit and lies all over again. He never wanted to help me. He claimed to love me genuinely but, it was yet another one of his cunning ploys to get me to submit to him and surrender my soul to him. All my attempts at expressing my hurt and anger was in vane because their method of bondage made it impossible for me to move. I couldn't understand why this was happening to me. I hadn't taken this man's money. It was C.J. who was now dead...and he took my baby with him!

Santiago walked towards the entrance of the room, turning to Dre.' "I expect you to do as I instructed. I have a few clients waiting on her now. They should be here by seven o'clock."

Dre' nodded his head as he looked out of the window, and then I heard the door close. *Clients waiting on me?* I tried to make sense of it. I was watching Dre.' I couldn't believe that I was thinking about how fine he was knowing all that I knew. I couldn't help it. He had this aura about him. I was completely under his spell. Maybe it was his tall frame...his muscular body. I was too tempted to explain. He walked closer to me...so close I could smell his cologne. It was the same as that day in the closet at his grandmother's house. I could see it in his eyes that he still had some feelings for me. I debated whether to use that to my advantage. What more did I have to lose? if he killed me...that would be perfect. *No more suffering.*

Tears rolled down my face at the thought of dying but, I already felt dead inside because I didn't have my baby anymore. Then it dawned on me. I'm pregnant. With all that was going on I forgot again. I knew I could definitely use *that* to my advantage. I mumbled Dre's name.

"If you scream Skylar, I will put the tape back on and

not take it off anymore." he warned me. I shook my head in agreement. The air felt so good going into my mouth. I couldn't hold back the tears.

"Dre,' why are you doing this to me? You know I didn't have anything to do with what C.J. did. You saw how he mistreated me."

He looked at me like he was concerned. I figured the tears would win him over. I needed to figure out how to break the news to him about the baby, and maybe he would let me go.

"Dre,' I have something to tell you." I said through tears. He sat on the edge of the hotel bed. "You can't kill me. You can't let them kill me. I'm pregnant."

He jumped up and lunged towards me. I closed my eyes and waited for the blow. He grabbed me by my neck, *"So you get down here and find you a nigga to be fucking and get pregnant? Who is it that nigga my sister saw you with?"* he demanded through clinched teeth.

The squeeze on my neck was getting tighter. I couldn't breath and was feeling light headed.

"Please, let me go." I tried saying through his tight grip on my neck. "It's your baby."

He let go of my neck and backed away from me. He put his hands over his head. "What do you mean? It can't be." he said looking confused.
"It is...and I'm sure." I tried saying through coughs.

"You have been the only man I've been with."

Hearing myself say that left me trying to wrap my mind around it too. I was pregnant by a man that was hired to kill me. I started to feel sick and I think Dre' saw it in my face. He ran over to me and picked up the chair I was tied to and took me to the bathroom and sat the chair in front of the toilet. I leaned in to the toilet and threw up. He returned me back to the sleeping area of the room while I was still tied to the chair. Dre' sat on the edge of the bed. I was at a loss for words. I had no idea what Dre' was going to do with me. A part of me was afraid...while the other part of me was unafraid. Everyone that I was close to was dead. I tried to convince myself that the baby wasn't a part of me.

I remembered the Pastor of the church saying everything that's good don't always come from God... that the devil will tempt you with good stuff to keep you bond by sin. I was a believer in God although I didn't know the word of God but, at that moment, I wondered why God would be taking me through this...why it seemed like HE was giving me the gun and telling me to pull the trigger...to get it over with. These things were difficult to understand. All I wanted was to have Carter back.

"Dre,' I love you. Why are you doing this to me? I thought you loved me? Or was that all a lie? When you made love to me, was that a lie? When you told me all your secrets, was that a lie? Or did you just know that I wouldn't live long enough to tell anyone? Why Dre'?

Why?"

He couldn't even look at me. Dre' walked over to the window which showcased the beautiful sky line. He slid open the patio door inviting the evening breeze inside. I watched him as he went back and forth with himself. I knew deep down, he loved me and didn't want to do this but, the devil had control of his soul too long for him to do any good. So, I prepared myself for what was to come.

There was a knock at the door. Dre' walked over and opened it allowing a woman inside. The two of them made eye contact as she came in. She was holding what looked to be a case of some sort. After placing the case on the table and opening it up, she pulled out a few lingerie pieces, makeup and hair products. "Hello Skylar. I'm Madalynn."

By her accent, I knew she was Cuban. She was pretty with exotic features. I was confused as to what she was about to do, and then it dawned on me as I remembered what Santiago said to Dre' about the clients being ready to see me at 7:00 pm. I began to scream and jerk around in my chair to loosen the restraints. Dre' immediately grabbed the duct tape and taped my mouth. No matter what sounds I made, no one could hear me. The woman pulled some powder out, put it on a cloth, and placed it underneath my nose. I tried holding my breath but, the tape over my mouth made it impossible. Immediately, I started to feel good. Everything around me seemed brighter and more alive. My head felt heavy my neck muscles relaxed and then it fell back. I stared up at the ceiling of the hotel room. The lights on the chandelier were dancing to music only I could hear. I felt extremely sexy and erotic. When I looked at Dre' he was staring at me. He looked even better than I thought before, and everything that I had gone through ceased to exist. All I wanted was to have Dre' make love to me. I could hear the woman and Dre' talking. "You can untie her now. She's not going anywhere. She inhaled all the powder I put on this cloth and won't give you any problems until it wears off. That probably won't be until late tomorrow when she wakes up. She will get tired at some point, and will pass out. When she does...just let her sleep it off but, make sure she's tied up because she will be distraught and wanting more of what I gave her."

"Why did you give her so much? She only has one client tonight." I heard Dre' ask.

The woman looked at him and smiled. "Well, she will go for hours. So, why don't we give her a head start?" She rubbed Dre's crouch. Dre' stepped back away from her and gave her a serious look. I watched in amusement and began to get aroused by seeing his reaction to her. I moaned to get their attention. Dre' walked over to me and looked me in my eyes. He was sexy, and I wanted him more than I ever had. Those eyes of his were looking straight into me. He took the tape off my mouth and I moved forward to try and kiss him but, he placed his hand over my mouth and shook his head. I smiled knowing I would win this battle. He untied my hands and feet, and then backed away from me. I looked at the women who was now sitting in a chair sipping a drink she had poured herself at the bar in the room. She smiled at me and I noticed how beautiful she was. I looked over her body and discovered she was sexy as hell. I wasn't into women, but, the powder she gave me, made everything seem sensual. I was so horny that I could feel the moisture between my legs. I walked towards Dre' and then stood in front of him. He looked down at me. I could smell his cologne...and that also made me want him more. Whatever the substance was; I never wanted it to ware off. It made my body feel so good. I tried to touch him but, he grabbed my wrist.

"You don't want me, Dre'?" I asked in a seductive voice. I could tell his resistance was low but, I was aware that I would need to make it even more tempting for him. They both watched me as I strutted over to the case. I pulled out some red bottom Louboutin's that just so happened to be my size. None of the lingerie looked to be appealing. So, I decided to wear the shoes and nothing else. I knew that would get Dre's attention because he loved my body. I began to take off all my clothes very slowly and put on the shoes. I watched Dre' as he watched me. I walked over to him. Even in the heels, I was slightly shorter than his 6-foot 1-inch frame. The powder had me feeling like I was someone other than myself. "Dre,' can you fuck me?" I looked at him straight in his eyes, and then I grabbed his hand. At first, he tried to resist me but, he couldn't escape me after I held his hand in mine.

CHAPTER 17

HIDDEN SECRETS

Dre'

This was not supposed to be happening like this. I knew I should've killed her when we were alone. When she held my hand in hers; I remembered how soft her skin was. As I looked at her body, I started to remember what I felt for her even though I was trying hard to remove those feelings after she shot me and left me for dead but, I couldn't resist her. I picked her up and she wrapped her legs around my waist. We kissed like the love we felt for each other never left.

Although I knew she had no idea what she was doing, and it was the drugs making her feel this way, I wanted to hold her in my arms and never let her go. I loved her, but I couldn't let myself get attached anymore. It would cost me my life. I laid her on the bed and took off my shirt. She smiled at the sight of me. I walked over to Madalynn who was watching us, and it turned me and Skylar on knowing that someone was watching. I grabbed the bottle of Patron that she was drinking and guzzled almost half of it down. I wasn't a drinker but, at that moment, I needed it. When I walked back over to Skylar, she was playing with herself and licking her fingers. I knew it had to be the drugs because Skylar was very shy. Even the times that we had sex before, she was never this freaky and relaxed. She always seemed frightened and anxious. The whole time she played with herself, her eyes never left Madalynn's. She was off limits for me but, not for Skylar. I motioned for her to come over to the bed. I sat in the recliner and watched Madalynn seduce Skylar. Skylar didn't look a bit surprised or scared...as if she has done this before. I watched as Madalynn kissed Skylar all down the side of her body and hips...and then between her thighs. I wasn't into girls on girls but, it really turned me on. Skylar kept her eyes closed the whole time. I knew the drugs were taking full effect of her behavior. When Madalynn looked at me, I motioned for her to leave. At that moment, I wanted Skylar all to myself. I couldn't resist her. She was so sexy. After Madalynn left, I watched Sky for a few minutes as she just squirmed around on the king-sized bed and played with herself. When she opened her eyes, her pupils were dilated. I knew the cocaine mixed with the African fly had her horny and high as a kite. The cocaine would probably ware off before that shit will. I watched her and thought about how beautiful she was when I saw her for the second time when her bruises healed. This could have really been something but, she couldn't just let C.J. go. I walked over to her and stood at the foot of the bed. When she opened her eyes again, she looked at me as if she didn't know who I was. She crawled to the edge of the bed and started kissing me on my stomach, and then made her way to my lips. There was something in her kiss. When I pulled away from her, she looked at me and jumped back as if she had seen a ghost. I turned to look behind me...and nothing was there.

"What's wrong, Skylar? You look like you've seen a ghost?"

"I did." she said. I knew it had to be the drugs making her act like that.

SKY

When I opened my eyes after kissing him, I thought I was going crazy. There were horns in the top of his head and his eyes were red like fire. Maybe, I was kissing the devil himself. I knew whatever was in that powder that women gave me was making me feel like this but, the thing was... I couldn't control my feelings. Something took over my body. Even though, in hindsight, I wanted him to stop...my body wanted more. I yearned for every part of him to connect with every part of me. I closed my eyes again and opened them to see Dre' was staring at me. "What do you mean that you saw a ghost?" he asked me over and over but, I didn't respond. "Skylar!" he screamed. But, I didn't answer. Instead, I kissed him slowly. His lips felt so good on top mine. I wanted him so bad...at least the drugs were making me think I did. He kissed me back, and I could tell from the bulge in his pants that he liked it. He kissed me on my neck and whispered in my ear, "I love you, Sky." I couldn't believe after all of this, he still wanted me. Or maybe it was just a front but, at that moment, I didn't care. All I wanted was him to make love to me. I laid back on the bed and spread my legs to invite him in. He stood there and stared at me as if I was someone else. The effects of the drugs were starting to make me dizzy and sleepy. The last thing I remembered was reaching my hand out for Dre.'

DRE'

I watched Skylar as she slept. Poor thing was so high she passed out. While she was sleeping, I tied her hands and feet up to the bed just in case the drugs wore off while she was sleeping. There was a knock at the door. I grabbed my Glock off the table and walked over to the door and looked out of the peep hole. It was the client that Santiago sent. When I opened the door, he smiled. "Hello, I'm looking for Candace." I looked him up and down. He looked like a Point Dexter ass nigga. I smirked because I knew he already paid Santiago for this service. "Unfortunately, Candace is not feeling well," I said. I opened the door so that he could look in and see Sky's naked body tied to the bed and passed out. "She took too much of the drugs Santiago gave her, so she won't be any use to you right now." He looked pissed. If I had spent the money he spent, I would be too. He walked away and pulled out his phone, I closed the door and went back into the room. My phone rung and I looked at it and knew exactly who it was. "DRE,' WHAT THE FUCK?" Santiago yelled in the phone. "Your girl you sent over drugged the hell out of her. Now, she is passed out on the bed." I tried to keep her awake until he came but, it wasn't looking good."

"DRE,' KILL THAT BITCH BY TOMORROW. NO SOONER! I WANT THE EFFECTS OF ALL THAT DRUG

TO BE WORN OFF! I WANT HER TO FEEL EACH BULLET. CALL ME WHEN ITS DONE. I'LL SEND MY GUYS TO CLEAN UP AND GET RID OF HER BODY. DRE,' DON'T FUCK WITH ME THIS TIME. I'M TIRED OF WAITING. I WANT HER DEAD... JUST LIKE HER FUCKING FATHER, THAT HOE ASS BOYFRIEND OF HERS, AND THEIR SON!"

He disconnected the call. I sat on the bed debating if I should do it then so that she wouldn't feel a thing. I stood up and screwed the silencer on my gun. I watched her as she slept I couldn't help but notice how beautiful she looked. I thought *if only we could have met under different circumstances.* She had been through so much and now she had to pay with her life for something that her father and bitch ass boyfriend did. I knew Skylar knew nothing about what happened to her father. All she knew was that he was murdered in a high-profile murder when she was nine years old. She had no idea that was the main reason Santiago wanted her dead. She was paying for the disloyalty of both her father and C.J. Every man in her life had hidden secrets that were coming back to haunt her. I couldn't bring myself to do it. I needed to go think and get some fresh air. I unscrewed the silencer off my gun and put it back in my pocket. After I grabbed my phone and walked to the door, I stopped and looked back at Skylar' who was still knocked out. I knew she wouldn't get away because I tied her securely to the bed. I walked over to her and taped her mouth in case she tried to scream if she woke up while I was gone. I walked back to the door, unlocked it, and then took another glance at Sky and walked out the door. When I got in the car, I punched the steering wheel out of anger. I was pissed at myself for loving her the way I did. I pulled off to go for a ride and think.

CHAPTER 18

EPIPHANY II

<u>SKY</u>

I woke up when I heard Dre's phone ringing. I knew it was Santiago by his heavy accented voice. Little did they know, I was ready for death. The sound of Santiago telling Dre' to kill me was actually a relief after all I'd been through. Losing my baby was the last straw. If the devil's plan was to make me lose my mind all the way, he accomplished that with my son's death. So, the sound of death was a sweet relief to my soul. I was lost in thought when I heard a small knock at the door. I fell silent because I knew it may have been someone Santiago sent although the invitation of death sounded pleasing. When I heard the door unlock and open, I closed my eyes and braced myself for the worst. I heard the footsteps coming toward me and then a voice of a woman with an Asian accent call my name. When I opened my eyes, it was a maid (a young Asian woman). I figured Santiago or Dre' sent her there to clean up the mess in the room. When I looked at her, she seemed shocked to see me naked and tied to the bed. At that moment, I knew that she wasn't sent by them. The thought of being able to escape with her help brought pleasure to me although I wanted to die. I started to moan so that she could take the tape off my mouth and I could convince her to untie me. She put her hand to her mouth signaling for me to be quiet, before she took the tape off my mouth and untied me.

"Skylar, I'm agent Carcetti with the FBI." she explained while pulling her badge out so that I could see it. "I'm going to untie you and explain to you what we're going to do. Put on this uniform so that you will look as if you work here." After she untied me, I dressed in the uniform and shoes that she had given me. I wasn't sure what was going on and was a little hesitant to believe her. *But what else could I do?* We walked towards the door and she opened it and looked out to make sure no one was there. She signaled for me to follow her. "Stay close behind me." She pulled out her phone and dialed, then explained to someone on the phone that she had located me and that we were headed toward them. I was so confused and unsure about whether I should believe her. I was also scared because I wasn't sure if Santiago had people watching the hotel.

When we made it down the elevator, we slipped into an employee only door which lead to the laundry room of the hotel. She opened a rear entrance door where shielded guards stood watch. I was sure they were Santiago's men until I saw FBI on their vests. I felt a sense of relief. One of the guards grabbed me and lifted me into the van. Everyone inside was quiet. I had so many questions. Obviously, my facial expression said it all.

"Skylar, we have been following Dre' and Santiago for a

long time. When we got word of their connection to you and C.J., we came up with a plan to get to them. It has been a challenge because of who Santiago is. He is a dangerous man. When you got on the plane to Atlanta, we had an agent on that plane to watch you. Reign was sent in to watch you."

When she said his name, my eyes got big. "Reign? The pilot from the plane?" I spoke in a low tone. I couldn't believe it. *Reign is FBI.*

"Skylar, I'm sorry about C.J. and your son. We tried to take them down before this but, as I said, Santiago is treacherous. We have been following him for years now. We lost him for a while, and then we got a tip about C.J.'s dealings with Santiago. After he had C.J. killed, we knew the only way to get him was through you because he wanted you dead." The Asian women explained.

I couldn't believe what I was hearing. I didn't know how to process all of this. I put my head in my hands and leaned down. The van suddenly stopped, and the Asian women stepped out of the van. When the door opened, Reign was standing there looking at me. I jumped up and ran to him.

"I'm so sorry, Skylar. It's over now. I promise," Reign said as he held me.

When we walked inside the building, there were cameras and people everywhere. The team of paramedics rushed me into a room where Robert and

Marilyn were. Marilyn ran to me and hugged me. I couldn't stop my tears. I sat in the chair and the paramedics checked me out. When I looked up, I saw the agents bringing in Dre', Santiago, and a bunch of other men in handcuffs. My body tensed. "Don't worry, they can't see you. It's a one-way mirror," Reign said as he walked into the room. After seeing the expression on my face, he walked over to me and held me. As Dre' walked passed, our eyes met...or so it seemed. Although I knew he couldn't see me, somehow his eyes found mine and my body tensed with fear. Reign felt me tense up and looked at me. *"Skylar, trust me, he will never hurt you again."* The crazy thing was, that wasn't what I was thinking. All I kept thinking was that I Loved him, I was in love with a man that wanted me dead.

As I cried in Reigns arms, I thought about the Epiphany I had when I found C.J.s body. I could hear God's voice saying, "I will give you another chance." At that moment, I knew death wasn't how he wanted my story to END.

And the LORD, he it is that doth go before thee; he will be with thee, he will not fail thee, neither forsake thee: fear not, neither be dismayed. – Deuteronomy 31:8, KJV

THE END...OR IS IT?

A Message from the Author

Hello,

First, I would like to give you a huge HUG straight through the pages of this book to Thank you for coming along this journey in part 2 of Skylar's story. As an Author I loveeeeeee to get feedback from the readers, to see what you guys thought of the books and how you felt while reading them. Writing Epiphany 1 & 2 definitely took me on an emotional roller coaster ride. I was angry, crying, laughing, sad, in my feelings all at the same time. What about you? Do you think Skylar's Story ends here? Should it end here? What about her and Dre's unborn child?

I would Love to see what you guys think will happen if there should be a part 3!

Turn to the next page to get all my social media handles. Tag me with a photo of you and the book and let me know your thoughts. Also, if you want to see your favorite character up close and personal? Comment and ask me how you can get access to the Short Film for Epiphany 1 and 2.

Ooh Yea! Don't forget to visit amazon to give me a review, every review helps to get me closer to bestseller.

MUAHHHH!!!! Thank you all sooo very much.

Instagram: @andreatrobinson

Instagram: theepiphanystory

Twitter: @AndreaTRobinson

Facebook: Andre'a T Robinson

Facebook: @TheEpiphanyStory

Snapchat: andreataniesha1

Email: epiphanythefilm@gmail.com

Amazon Author page:
https://www.amazon.com/Andrea-T-Robinson/e/B01BKWUBQE

Made in the USA
Columbia, SC
01 November 2018